THE GOLEM

I call him Golly, to make him seem less scary. He's only a little over five feet tall, but he's much bulkier than any regular person you're likely to meet, unless you hang around in some awfully odd places. His skin, which is synthetic, is colorless; also he has no hair, not even eyebrows. He hasn't got much in the way of a neck, either.... He's not really alive, he's awfully strong and fast, and he's not afraid of anything.

All the transit centers keep one around for emergencies. I removed his clear plastic wrapping and pressed the button that says ACTIVATE ...

"VINTAGE ZELAZNY!"
School Library Journal

ROGER ZELAZNY

A DARK TRAVELING

Illustrated by Lebbeus Woods

MILLENNIUM

A BYRON PREISS BOOK

AVON BOOKS ▲ NEW YORK

AVON BOOKS
A division of
The Hearst Corporation
105 Madison Avenue
New York, New York 10016

Book design based on hardcover book design by Alex Jay/Studio J
Hardcover cover design by Alex Jay
Hardcover cover painting by Lebbeus Woods
Logo design by Lebbeus Woods
Book edited by David M. Harris
Millennium Books and the Millennium symbol are trademarks
of Byron Preiss Visual Publications, Inc.
Special thanks to Kirby McCauley and Elisabeth Wansbrough

First Avon Books Printing: May 1989

To Cathy Cavanagh
in particular
and all of the other teachers
at Rio Grande School
in Santa Fe
who taught my children
to enjoy reading

PROLOGUE

The candle's flame was a bright leaf. Beyond the window a full moon hung in the evening sky. The house was absolutely still.

She stared into the flame, where many pasts swam, along with a multitude of presents and a confusion of futures. With practice these could be sorted, however, and she had had a lot of practice.

She forgot the house. She did not see the moon. After a time she was not even aware of the flame. Only the images held her attention; pasts, presents, and futures were shuffled like cards. . . .

She smiled faintly. A past, then. A true past of this place, for anchorage. . . .

. . . *The man had laid out the rods and rolled the brass wheels. Now he walked, the wheels still clicking in his hand, his dark cloak and the feather in his hat undisturbed by any wind. His path led him through a place of whiteness, as if snow were banked at either hand. But the whiteness churned slowly, drifting. Mist, fog . . . He moved like a phantom through the pale places. Before him, finally, there came a lessening, a fading. Faint outlines were beginning to take form. He did not change his pace,*

3

however, but continued on his way. Abruptly the mists were gone and the outlines sprang into full relief. The man stopped in a grassy area next to a road, regarding the distant prospect of a great city, its towers gleaming in the light of early day. Overhead something was descending toward an unseen destination, something large and metallic, its wings unflapping. As he watched, a metal vehicle with no visible means of propulsion passed rapidly along the road to his left.

"Sapristi!" the man exclaimed.

After a time, he began walking again.

She nodded, and the image faded, to be replaced by another. Futures, now . . .

. . . A lithe, dark-haired man clad in black was rising to his feet, a silver earring glistening on the lobe of his left ear. His hair was long and black, secured behind his head. He was smiling as he raised his hands before him, and she felt that they held death. They were reaching directly toward her.

". . . And his name is Crow."

The words flowed unbidden into her mind. She shuddered. Better to shuffle this one away. It was too menacing, and she did not want it to come to be. Pass on.

Try Now . . .

. . . The walls of an arroyo slid past at a dizzying rate, small dark outlines she knew to be piñon and juniper trees passed at either hand. She sensed the runner's controlled breathing. The big moon cast shadows within the pale

*glow it had spread across the land. There was
something wild, almost frantic in the movements of the boy who ran and ran. Now he
threw his head back, and his mouth was open.
His pace did not slacken, however.*

She sighed, for she knew that this meant she
would be subjected to loud rock music before
too long. Brothers can be so trying. . . .

*. . . Then there was the power station, its
vibrating towers haloed in blue, dark conduits
like sea serpents coiled about their feet. A small
army was camped before the installation, facing a range of hills, where another army held
its position. An occasional flash of light occurred within one camp or another. Nothing
here had changed. Time to move closer, to try
for a contact—*

Abruptly, the scene vanished. Puzzled, she
tried summoning it again. It took form slowly,
hovered an instant, then vanished once more.
Again she tried. This time it did not come at
all. She shook her head. It was not the first
time she had encountered this phenomenon.
Later.
More Now . . .

*. . . A body garbed in a white gi passed
through the air above the hip of another gi-clad
figure, a dark belt about its waist. She sensed
rather than heard the cry that accompanied
this. The figure landed upon the mat, arm slap-
ping simultaneously at a forty-five degree angle
out to the side. Barry was at it again. . . .*

*   *   *

Unbidden, a new image occurred. . . .

. . . Dead. A city of broken buildings. Dust blowing along its littered streets. Heaps of rubble at every hand. No window left unshattered. Nothing stirring but the wind and the dust. . . .

It began to fade just as an almost familiar figure rounded a corner. She let it go. She had not called for this one.

Then she realized that it had been a future rather than a present and she swore softly. She should probably have tried holding it for a better look.

She relaxed and continued to watch. . . .

. . . A wolf was running through a forest. . . .

She watched for a long while, but that was all there was to it. As monotonous as watching Jim running back in the arroyos. She dismissed the wolf. Nothing useful there. She tried again for the two armies, and the vision came and went and stayed away.

Suddenly she saw Tom, next door, down in the transcomp room, puttering with the machinery. She became aware that something was rushing toward him. From where, she did not know. What it was, she could not make out. But she knew that it was threatening and that it was on its way, right now, this minute, and she cried out, though she knew that he could not hear her. In that instant everything she had seen flowed together into a single general vision. She did not understand it, but for a moment she felt its connectedness.

She screamed, and the image went away and

the candle went out. Only the pattern remained, signifying menace, overlaid with her sudden fear. But despite the fear she was on her feet and running, out the door, down a hallway, toward a stair. . . .

Smoking candle. Empty room.

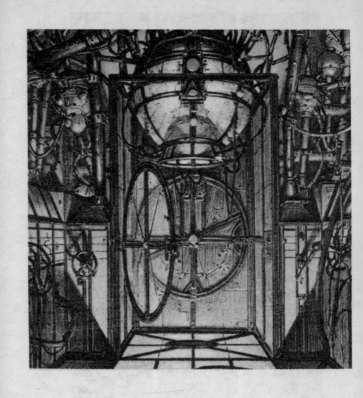

I

My father was the keeper of the Eddystone Light . . . Know that song? If you don't, it doesn't matter. It's just that it always reminds me of home.

I'm a normal fourteen-year-old boy, my name is James Wiley, and I live in a large building in a southwestern state capital in the United States. My sister Becky is a witch, my older brother Dave lives in a castle, and our exchange student Barry is a trained assassin. I also have an uncle named George who is a werewolf. And my own palms do get itchy whenever there's a full moon, so I guess I have some of the same genes. It *must* be the genes. I try to be scientific about these matters, because I'm going to be a scientist one of these days.

Unfortunately, there was a full moon for a while earlier that evening. That's when the trouble began, and, of course, I wasn't home. I'd smeared on the cortisone cream Dr. Holmes had prescribed for what he called my "monthly palmar dermatitis," and it was working okay. But I also get restless on these occasions, and I take long walks in the arroyos out back. Well, I jog through them usually. But don't misunderstand. I don't change shape or anything like that. I don't even howl much.

I came in from my moonlight jog sweaty and very hungry—the same as always. The first thing I do at such times is raid the refrigerator. Then I take a shower. Then I put on more cream. Then I go to my room and play loud music and pace. This usually irritates Becky, whose room is two doors up the hall from mine, because whenever there's a full moon she turns out the lights in her room and stares at a candle flame for hours. She's weird.

I did not get as far as all that this time, though. I came in the back way, remembering the hamburger in the meat drawer, and Becky was waiting for me right by the door and she was holding a brown paper bag in her left hand and looking upset. Now, Becky is a tough little blond thing and she is somewhere around my age, maybe even a little older—fifteen, say— and it had been a long time since I'd seen her upset about anything. So when she said, "Come on!" and grabbed hold of my hand and turned away I followed her.

She led me through our part of the building and over to the heavy metal door that separates us from the foundation headquarters. Then she released me and stuck her right hand into the bag she was carrying. A moment later I heard a very suspicious *click* as she raised the bag and pointed it at the door.

"Becky!" I said. "What have you got in that bag?"

"You already guessed," she said, her voice steady. "Just listen to me, Jim. I want you to go over to my left, reach across and unbolt the door, then give it a push and get back out of the way."

"You've got to be kidding," I said. "You mean

you're going to start blazing away when that door opens?"

"Only if something tries to come through it," she said.

"Uh, I don't know where you got it, but I think you'd better let me have the gun."

"Nope," she said. "Because you might freeze up, and I know I won't."

I looked at her narrowed green eyes, at her tight shoulders, and I thought of some things about her that I hadn't thought of for a long time. I knew then that she could do it if it needed doing, and I wasn't all that sure I could.

"Okay," I said, and I moved into position, unfastened the door and gave it a push.

I stepped back fast, and a few moments later I sighed, for there was nothing there, nothing waiting to rush through and do us harm. I hadn't realized until then that I'd been holding my breath.

The light was on in the hallway and there was no one in sight in either direction. No unusual sounds came to us, either. There was a foreign human odor, though. Also blood.

"Now can you tell me what's going on?" I asked.

"If only Barry were here," she answered.

Great! Nothing like it to make you feel important. *If only Barry were here*. He was not here, of course, because he was off at a dojo, kicking, blocking, and punching. Or was it the other dojo? In that case he'd be throwing, grappling, locking. Whatever, he was off practicing those things Becky wanted him for now, things I gather he'd started doing at about the time he'd learned to walk. It irritated me that she talked about him as if he were an adult and still treated me like a kid. After all, he was only a year older than me.

Becky moved forward, throwing switches, lighting the way ahead. I followed her along the hallway to the right, which led to the reception area, peering into two vacant offices we passed.

I halted at the desk, behind which hung the sign reading TRANSIT FOUNDATION.

"Well, Barry *isn't* here," I said. "So I think you'd better tell me about it. I've already smelled blood."

She turned suddenly then, beneath the big picture of Leonardo da Vinci standing with his back to a table on which a mess of brass gears and shafts is strewn. The corner of some construction juts from behind his left arm. He is smiling faintly. It is a self-portrait. It is not in any of the art books. No one has ever spotted it for what it was.

"Shh!" Becky said, raising one finger to her lips. Then she whispered, "Just wait a bit!"

I nodded, and she turned away and I followed her. We inspected two more offices, a small conference room, and a coatroom. They were all, mercifully, empty. But I was already pretty sure of that, by sniffing.

We came to the foot of the stairs and she looked up into the darkness and shuddered. The smells were present here also.

"I can't!" she said softly. "I can't—go upstairs."

I put my hand on her shoulder.

"You don't have to," I said. "Do you?"

She continued to stare into the darkness.

"I guess not," she said. "There's probably nothing . . . really there. Not now."

"I wish I knew what was going on."

"Come on," she said at last. "I'll show you."
And, "I'm sorry," she added.

"What do you mean?"

"Just come," she said, leading me away from
the stair in the direction of the small storeroom to the rear of the building.

I wanted to scream but I followed her instead. A nasty movie had begun playing in my
mind and I couldn't switch it off. I'd been telling myself all along that she'd just heard a few
noises and gotten nervous.

She led me into the storeroom, which was
lit. We made our way past mops and buckets, a
rack full of cleaning compounds, and a stack of
folding chairs to the place where she began to
fiddle with the hidden latch. A moment later a
section of the wall swung away from us, revealing a short, narrow flight of stairs leading
downward. This corridor was also illuminated,
by an overhead fixture, and there was a metal
door at its end. The hidden room behind the
metal door was actually above ground level,
despite the descent, because of the slope of the
land. It was a windowless border place, de-
signed so that anybody connected with the foundation who glanced out a window at that odd
corner would think it a part of our living quarters next door, if they thought about it at all.
And vice versa, if we had guests. We haven't
had many, though, since my mother's death
earlier in the year.

I followed Becky down the steps and up to
the door.

"Are we going to do that SWAT team business again?" I whispered.

She just shook her head and pushed the door
open.

I followed her into the transcomp room. The lights were on, and the place was a mess. Becky slumped into a metal folding chair, handed me the paper bag, and began to cry.

I looked around, and I saw a stain on the floor, over by the main console. I already knew what it was before I crossed the room and stopped to examine the smear. My sense of smell is abnormally acute, and it's even better on nights such as that one. I could tell that my father had been in here earlier, and I could tell that blood had been shed. I could have told these things with the lights out. There was also the stranger's odor, which I had detected upstairs.

When I rose I looked again at the transcomp, and I saw a place where it had been damaged. It was still switched on and humming faintly, but only one of the indicator lights was burning. Something had obviously shorted out when it had been bashed. I reached over and flipped the power switch to off.

The logbook lay on the floor. I picked it up, smoothed some bent pages, and read the latest entry. Dad had signed in a little over an hour ago. That was all. No mention of what bands he'd be running or anything like that. I replaced the book on its shelf and looked in the drawer where he kept his revolver. The drawer was already partly open, and, of course, there was no gun there, because it had to be in the bag I was holding.

I reached into the bag and removed the thing carefully. Yep. I held the weapon he normally kept in the drawer, easing the hammer back into position and popping the cylinder. I already knew that it had been fired, from the smell. I was curious, though. . . . Yes. One round had been discharged. Then I closed it again, not sure whether to put it back in the drawer or to keep holding it until I knew what had happened.

"Where'd you find the gun?" I asked Becky.

"On the floor," she said, "over there," and she pointed to the far corner of the room.

"What were you doing down here anyway?"

"I was in my room meditating," she said, "and I kept getting these feelings that something terrible was going to happen. Then I heard the gunshot. So I ran downstairs and I listened by the door for a while. But I didn't hear anything else. Finally I opened the door and I came on down. The place was empty and looked just the way it does now—except for the gun," she added, gesturing again.

"So what did you do?"

"I picked up the gun and put it in a paper bag I saw in the wastebasket—because I didn't want to touch it any more than I had to. But if something really bad was going on I thought I might need it. Then I went back upstairs and over to our place, and I locked the door. I went to the kitchen after that and waited for you."

"You said you knew that the shot came from here," I stated. "How could you tell? It would be pretty muffled down here. It could as easily have been from somewhere outside."

She shook her head.

"Tom had just gone over," she said. "He told me he was going right before he went. Then about five minutes later I heard the shot. The timing was just right for him to have gotten down here, turned everything on, and logged in."

I licked my lips, which felt very dry, and I nodded. Tom Wiley is my father. He is not Becky's father, though, so she calls him by his first name instead of Dad or something like that. It's the way they worked it out between them.

"Did he say anything about what he planned on doing here?" I asked.

"No."

"Did he get any phone calls or visitors before he came over?"

"I didn't hear the phone ring," she answered, "or the doorbell either. Why?"

"I was trying to figure whether he was attacked from this side or some other."

"Oh. I never thought of that."

"In fact, a whole bunch of odd questions come to mind," I said. "First, whose blood is that on the floor? Dad's? Or the other guy's?"

"I'd guessed it was Tom's," she said. "If he'd hurt the other guy there would be no reason for him to run away. He'd have a wounded prisoner—or a corpse. Hey! Maybe he killed the guy and took the body away with him to get rid of the evidence somewhere."

"I don't think so," I said. "If that had been the case he'd be back by now. It's been over an hour."

"Could they have been fighting and gotten into the field and both been transitted out?" she asked.

I gestured at the console. "Then how could the machine have gotten damaged after they were gone?"

"Okay. I'm not thinking clearly," she said. "But what are we going to do?"

I glanced back up the stairway.

"You're right. We'd better do something. I'll save my other questions for later. Come on."

"Where?"

"We're going to close up here," I said. "Leave everything just the way it is for now. Then we're going back next door and I'm going to wake up the Golem."

"Do I have to be there when you do it?" she asked. "I don't like the thing at all."

"I know," I told her. "But it has to scan you while I press the button, so it'll know you're okay and leave you alone."

"But Tom did that that one other time—"

"Yes, but it has to be reprogrammed each time it's turned on. It does work for *us*, though, you know. Besides, I'm going to bring it over here to patrol the place. You won't even have to look at it then."

"I know, but— Okay, let's get it over with."

We turned out the light, closed the door, and started up the stairway.

"Your face looks dirty," she said.

"That shouldn't make any difference to a Golem," I told her.

II

We stopped on the way and hung the CLOSED sign in the window of the front entrance. I was afraid I'd forget to do it later, and I was sure that it would not be business as usual tomorrow. I realized as I did it that I should get on the phone and call Mrs. Dell, the secretary, and ask her to get in touch with everyone on the staff and tell them not to come in. As I decided this it also occurred to me that I should check the appointment book and see whether anyone was scheduled to stop by tomorrow. They should also be phoned and told to make it another time.

Damn! There was suddenly so much to do, and I was sure I hadn't thought of everything.

We returned to our side of the building and locked the door behind us. Then we climbed the stairs to the second floor and went into Dad's bedroom. Becky hung back at the doorway while I crossed to the area in front of the closet and rolled back the rug.

I caught hold of the recessed ringbolt and pulled upward on it. The door in the floor creaked open, and I heard Becky say, "Oh!"

I didn't blame her, actually, because Golly still scares me a little, even though I've done maintenance work on him and I know I'm safe so long as I do what I'm supposed to.

I start calling him Golly whenever I'm near him, possibly to make him seem less like something on a late night scare show. He's only a little over five feet tall, but he's much bulkier than any regular person you're likely to meet, unless you hang around in some awfully odd places. His skin, which is synthetic, is colorless; also, he has absolutely no hair, not even eyebrows. He hasn't got much in the way of a neck either, and his hands and feet are very large. He kind of reminds me of a short, mean-looking Mr. Clean. He's not really alive, he's awfully strong and fast, and he's not afraid of anything. All of the transit centers have one just like him around somewhere, in case of emergencies.

I knelt and removed the clear plastic wrapping covering him. He didn't stir, of course. He doesn't even breathe. I unzipped the top of his black jumpsuit and opened the panel on his chest.

When I pressed the button that says ACTIVATE he opened his very blue eyes, sat up, and then stood. He remained in that position and would continue to do so until he received further instructions.

I stood directly in front of him and pressed the PASS button. This was followed by a faint click from behind the panel.

"Okay, Becky," I said. "You've got to come here for a minute."

She didn't answer, and when I turned and looked she was simply staring at Golly.

"I can't," she said. "You'll have to come and get me."

"Okay," I answered, and I went over and took her hand.

I led her back and she squeezed my hand very hard the whole way. As soon as I'd pushed the button and gotten another *click* she let go and backed away fast.

"We're safe now," I said, hitting FOLLOW. "He knows we're okay."

Then I took hold of Golly's hand, which feels something like a rubberized raincoat, and gave a slight tug. He responded by stepping up out of his storage cell and following me for a few paces. I left him to go back and close the hatch and to restore the rug to its former position. He stood stock-still while I did this. When I returned to guide him again Becky was already waiting out in the hall.

He followed me along like a child, his grip strangely gentle, moving soundlessly on his large bare feet. Becky walked so that I was always positioned between Golly and her.

When we reached the downstairs hallway I heard a knocking sound coming from the metal door. It struck me that it might have been going on as a kind of background noise for some time, and that I'd been partly aware of it while I was occupied upstairs.

Somehow I didn't think that the one we were worried about would be knocking. Sneaking about, yes. Knocking, no.

So I called out, "Who's there?"

"Bill Jeeter," came the reply from beyond the door, "with your cleaning service. I came in the back way and I just now saw your sign out front. I wanted to know if you'd be needing us tomorrow night."

"No," I said, thinking fast. "I think they're planning some remodeling. In fact, it would be better if you don't clean tonight either. It'll just get messed up again."

There followed a moment of silence, then, "I'll still have to bill you for coming out," he said.

"That's okay," I answered. "I'm sorry they didn't notify you."

"Me, too," he answered gruffly, and I heard something like the rattle of a bucket handle. "Tell them to call when they want us back, will you?"

"I will," I said, and again, "Sorry."

I heard the rattle once more and the sound of footsteps going away.

I sighed.

"It's hard to think of everything," I said.

Becky glanced at Golly.

"Now what?" she asked.

"We have to give them time to clear out," I said, "before I set him to patrolling in there."

I opened the closet door, led Golly inside, and left him.

"Do you really think there could still be someone else here?" she asked.

"Maybe upstairs next door," I said. "Maybe not, too. But I don't want to go and look. As soon as it's clear, Golly can go and check the place out. If there's someone there, he'll capture whoever it is and we can question him."

"Or it," she said. "You still haven't said why you think someone would still be there after this much time."

"The transcomp was broken, and it had to be done from this side. That means someone had to be there to break it. And that means that person couldn't use it afterward to get away himself."

"Or itself," she said. "I see what you mean. So it's either still in there somewhere or it's taken off outside."

"I think so," I said, turning away and heading for the kitchen. I was still starved.

"So where's Tom?" she asked.

"I think he was hurt but got away through the machine," I told her. "Whoever was responsible couldn't follow for one reason or another. So he damaged the equipment so no one else could follow Dad either."

"Stranding himself here?"

"Yes."

"Why?"

"I don't know," I answered as I opened the refrigerator. "But I'm sure nothing good is involved."

I opened the meat drawer and located the package of hamburger.

"So why not the other way around?" she asked.

"What do you mean?"

"Say the attacker got away and Tom fell against the equipment and damaged it. Then he crawled off and . . ." Her voice faded.

I shook my head.

"Doesn't make sense," I answered. "He'd have come back here or headed for the nearest telephone. Or we'd have found him down there. No reason for him to crawl off and hide."

"Yes," she said, nodding slowly. "I guess you're right. Unless neither one was able to get away through the machine and whoever it was kidnapped Tom."

"You said you got down there pretty fast after you heard the shot, didn't you?" I asked.

"Yes."

"Did you hear anyone leaving?"

"No, I didn't."

I shrugged.

"Gee, that's gross—to eat raw hamburger that way."

"I like it like this."

"Hey! That's not dirt on your face. It's—"

We heard the front door open and close. Simultaneously, we both looked at the brown paper bag on the table.

But a moment later I heard a scream, and I knew that it was all right. It was not just any scream. It was a *kiai*, the kind of yell martial artists give when they attack.

I rushed out of the kitchen, heading for the front hall.

"It's all right, Barry!" I cried, just as another *kiai* sounded. "Barry! It's okay!"

I reached the hall in time to see Barry kick Golly in the stomach. Of course nothing happened. I hadn't activated the system that would have caused him to fight back. Golly just stood there in the closet and absorbed the blow without stirring.

"Honest, it's okay," I said. "Your people must have a Golem back home."

"That's a Golem?" he asked, stepping back and staring. "I've heard them mention it, but I'd never seen the thing."

"That's a Golem," I said.

He picked a light jacket up off the floor.

"I was just going to hang this up," he explained. "He . . . kind of surprised me. What's he doing in the closet, anyway?"

Barry is my height, but he's a lot heavier in the shoulders. His hair is straight and brown, a couple of shades lighter than mine, and his

eyes are hazel. His movements are very grace-
ful, almost like a dancer's, and I've seen him
break bricks with his hands.

"We were waiting for the cleaning service to
leave before I sent him in next door," I said.

"I didn't see their truck when I came up," he
stated.

"Good," I said. "They're gone. In that case
I'll do it now."

I took Golly's hand and led him out of the
closet, pausing to press PASS for Barry. Then I
guided Golly to the metal door.

"What's going on?" Barry asked.

"Wait till I get this done and I'll tell you all
about it," I said.

I opened the door and took Golly inside. I led
him back and around to the foot of the stairway.
Then I opened the panel on his chest and pressed
the PATROL button. My finger hesitated for a
moment over the KILL button; I moved it and
pressed SUBDUE. I stepped aside and watched
him mount the stairs.

"Hey, you need a shave," Barry said.

"Huh?" I asked, rubbing my chin. "I just
shaved last month." It did feel kind of fuzzy.
"It's the full moon," I said.

"So what are you sending that—thing—after?"
he asked.

"Let's go back to the kitchen," I said. "I'll
tell you while I finish eating. We've got a lot to
do."

We cut through the reception area on the
way back. Another glance at the portrait hang-
ing there set me to thinking. . . .

There was a time in the middle of the eigh-
teenth century when French possessions blocked
westward expansion of English colonies in

America. If England had not won the Seven
Years War, North America might well have
been divided very differently than it is today,
with a New England in the East, a New France
in the middle, and a New Spain out West.
Supposing England had not won the Seven
Years War and that *somewhere* this situation
prevails?

Supposing Cortés's tiny, lucky band of troops
had not been quite so lucky and the Aztecs had
not been conquered . . .

Supposing the Russians had decided not to
sell Alaska to the United States . . .

Supposing Charles Martel had lost the Battle of Tours back in the eighth century, and
Muslim troops had swept on up into Europe.
Might we have a copy of the Koran rather
than a Gideon Bible in hotel rooms today?

Supposing there had been an all-out atomic
war and there were no humans left alive . . .

Supposing the Crusades had not occurred, or
had gone differently . . .

Or go way back, and suppose the last Ice
Age had lasted longer, or ended sooner. Or
supposing humans had developed different abilities than those they have now and had learned
magic rather than, say, calculus . . .

Supposing that each of these possibilities were
true, and many others as well, and that somewhere there is a world, a whole version of
reality, where this is exactly the case. Supposing all of these worlds run together, side by
side, parallel, as it were, emerging from their
various decision points in history and prehistory.
Supposing a transit device were possible, a
means of tuning into and traveling among these
versions of reality, these parallel worlds. If

enough worlds existed, it would seem that there would be one or more where such a device was discovered.

Supposing it had happened here—say, back around the time of the Renaissance. And supposing it was realized that while full exposure to these other bands of reality would be disastrous to our entire civilization, a limited exposure could be of great benefit . . .

Supposing only a few individuals existed on each such world—a family, perhaps—who possessed the means of transit and were responsible for the commerce among these bands of reality. Supposing a necessity for secrecy led them to assume the appearance of something other than what they were—say, perhaps, a think tank, a foundation . . .

One might also suppose that these families would become related over the years, that there would be frequent visits and even something like a student exchange program for the kids.

Just supposing, of course.

Barry comes from a pretty tough place. My sister Becky is a witch. My brother Dave currently lives in a castle. I also have an uncle named George who is a werewolf.

I've done a lot of visiting but I haven't done my hitch as an exchange student yet. I get my turn after Dave comes back.

III

We call them "bands," these parallel worlds, after the areas on the transcomp's control indicator where we tune the transit field. The word transcomp, by the way, refers to the partnership of a transit machine with a computer—a situation which makes the work an awful lot easier than it was in the old days, back before computers were available. Of course, we had our computer several generations before anyone else did in this band, so we've been calling it a transcomp for a pretty long time.

Just as computers were developed in another band before they were developed here, Golly comes from yet another band, where they've long been expert at building androids—which is what he is, a soft robot.

There are a dozen-plus parallel worlds with which we do varying amounts of business. We call these the "lightbands." Then there are a number of bands that we know about, where we have observers in residence, but where we do nothing other than watch. For most of these—some of them recently discovered—we either do not know enough yet to try to be of help, or it has been determined that any interference on our part at this point in their development might do more harm than good. We call these the "graybands."

Then there are a few worlds where things went very wrong and there are no people left alive. These are the "deadbands." We have learned a lot from them, though, just as we have from the graybands. And this makes us very careful about what we allow to cross from one band to another.

And there is one more category: the "darkbands." There are three of them. Once there was only one. The inhabitants of that one have no scruples against interfering grossly in the normal development of other worlds, in exploiting their people, their resources, their technologies. They may well even be responsible for some of the deadbands. And that brings things full circle. For the lightbands were inadvertently responsible for the first darkband, a long time ago. In their zeal to help a developing world along, the lightbands had given too much of a good thing too soon to a promising civilization—including transit technology—with a disastrous effect upon its culture. We learned an expensive lesson from that darkband, and that is why we have been very, very careful in these matters ever since.

I have visited the graybands, the deadbands, and all but one of the lightbands. Seeing something of them all is considered a necessary part of one's education, in the families. We also study the histories of each of them, which is why I can be so glib when it comes to making up examples involving decision points and parallel worlds. Having to learn your own history is rough enough; having to learn a whole bunch of them is that much harder. The worst ones to learn are the ones which are the most similar to your own. But it does teach you a certain facility in playing games with the past.

I might add that I've never visited a darkband. But that's okay with me. I get the impression that we maintain covert agents in those places and that they do the same with us. But there is no normal commerce with them.

We talked about these matters in the kitchen after we'd filled Barry in on what had occurred. It seemed a reasonable conclusion that a darkband had to be behind what had happened, zeroing in on our equipment and waiting for it to be activated. Barry thought it possible that they had wanted to abduct a lightband transit operator in order to obtain some piece of technical information or other concerning our operations. He felt that Dad might well now be a darkband prisoner.

When I said that they couldn't have taken him away with the equipment damaged, he pointed out that whoever had come through could have brought a portable transit unit with him, smashed ours after subduing my father, and departed with him by means of his own gear—effectively isolating us and preventing us from notifying the other lightbands for a time. This thought had not occurred to me, and it depressed me even more than the guesses I had made so far.

I had assumed that whatever was going on was a part of something directed against our entire band rather than any particular individual. I thought this because of penetrations they had attempted in the past, elsewhere. Also, I found myself wanting to believe that Dad had escaped, because it gave us a chance of finding him, whereas I didn't know what we could do if he were a darkband prisoner.

I kept on eating while we talked. It sounds callous, but I couldn't help it. My metabolism just gets wild at certain times, and this was one of those occasions.

"Either he left by means of our equipment or he didn't," I said.

Barry nodded.

"If he didn't, we can't be sure where he is," I continued.

"If he did use our equipment, it should still be set at the transit band he went out on!" he said.

"Unless it got jiggled," Becky added, "when it was damaged. Weren't you just telling me the other day how sensitive that tuner is?"

I nodded.

"But not all of the bands are close together," I said. "If it's in the vicinity of one that's at a pretty isolated frequency, that will be enough."

"But some of them *are* close together," Barry said.

I put the empty plastic tray into the trash. My hunger was finally gone.

"It's kind of silly to talk about it," I said, "when we can go and look in a few minutes."

"Let's go and look now," he said, reaching for the paper bag in the middle of the table.

"Let Golly finish his search," I told him.

"I'm not afraid to go in there."

"I'm sure you're not," I said, wondering whether he ever dropped that macho business. He'd been living with us for five months now, and he always seemed to have a bit of a chip on his shoulder. "But it's his job, and I've got to go and call Mrs. Dell anyway." I rubbed my chin. "I might even shave," I added. "Maybe you ought to eat something, too, while you're waiting. You might need some extra energy later."

He thought a moment, smiled, and nodded again. "You may be right," he said. "Okay. Go and call her. I'll grab some calories."

I did that thing, and it turned out that she remembered the appointments list also, and said she'd call everybody. When she asked for how long we'd be shut down I didn't know what to tell her, though. So I said that we'd have to let her know. Of course, she realized that something unusual was afoot, and since she isn't in on family secrets I wasn't quite certain what to say when she asked, "What's the matter, Jim? What's going on?"

"Well, it's"—and I remembered the magic word—"classified," I said.

"Oh," she replied. "Well, I hope everything's all right."

"It may be soon," I said. "I don't know yet."

"Is there anything I can do to help?"

"No," I told her. "Thanks. We appreciate it. We'll call you as soon as things are straightened out. Goodbye."

I hung up, hoping that that took care of the remaining loose ends, and I went upstairs and got out the electric razor Dad had given me for a birthday present. I'd only needed to use it a few times, but when I looked in the mirror I could see that it was time to plug it in again. Funny. I hadn't noticed I'd looked all that fuzzy this morning when I was brushing my teeth, but the full moon effects had been getting stronger in recent months, and I'd a strong feeling it was tied in with this.

I had just finished and had opened a bottle of after-shave stuff I had also been given—deciding against using it, because it irritated my nose—when I heard a scream from next door. I ran the length of the hall and took the stairs like a mountain goat. It was a man's voice, and since Golems are voiceless it meant that Golly had just surprised someone and was in the process of doing the SUBDUE bit. And since the cleaning service had departed, it seemed to me that *this* could be our man, poking around, trying to get into the locked files or the safe, where some pretty sensitive materials might be found. Of course. It was the logical thing for a darkband intruder to do—try to steal our secrets to learn what it was that we wanted to introduce into this society at this time to strengthen it, increase its flexibility, make it too strong for them to be able to exploit.

So I ran. Not just because I was eager to see what he looked like, but because I wanted to get there before Barry did. Maybe I was misjudging him, but that warrior society in which he'd grown up had a pretty stern code in some life-and-death matters, and I was afraid if he got it into his head he was protecting Becky and me we might not get a chance to talk to the prisoner. On the other hand, the head of a household is a strong authority figure where he comes from, and with Dad and Dave gone, I was in charge. If I could just get there in time and remind him of this I'd a feeling things would be all right.

I heard another scream; also some interesting profanity. It sounded as if it came from upstairs next door and to the rear.

When I reached the downstairs hallway I

saw that Barry was already at the door, opening it. And he carried the paper bag in his left hand. Becky was nowhere in sight. I raced toward him.

"Barry!" I called. "Wait!"

But he'd already gone through the entrance.

I reached it and passed inside. I turned, then, and headed along the hallway to the rear. There came another outburst from upstairs, and the voice sounded vaguely familiar.

As I turned the corner into the rear hallway, I caught sight of Barry starting up the stairs, his right hand plunged into the bag.

"I'm in charge here, Barry, when my Dad is gone!" I yelled. "And I said *stop!*"

He slowed and looked at me.

"Wait up, damn it!" I added.

He halted and sighed.

"I'm better fit to handle this thing, Jim," he said.

"Probably so—if we do it your way," I answered, finally reaching the foot of the stairs and turning. "But don't. You'll blow our cover."

"What do you mean?" he asked as I began climbing.

"I mean that the bird is flown," I said softly. "The smell is gone, and I recognize that voice. You might have, too, if you'd paid more attention. You keep that weapon in the bag and don't do anything that'll make this even harder for me to explain."

"Uh, sure, Jim," he said almost meekly. "I didn't—"

I hurried past him and turned left when I reached the head of the stairs. I made for the library, then, which is also the main conference room, because that's where it seemed the sounds were coming from.

Through the open entrance I could see that the lights were turned on. The sounds of scuffling had ceased, but the voice I'd recognized was now pleading rather than cursing or shouting.

"Let me go, will you? That hurts. Why won't you answer me? I—"

I ran into the room and saw where Golly held a man sprawled face downward on a tabletop while he twisted his arm up behind his back with one hand and pushed on his shoulder with the other.

This was a very good position—for me, that is, not for the man who was in it. It was good because he couldn't see what I was doing as I unzipped the top of Golly's jumpsuit, opened the panel, pushed PASS, closed the panel, and drew the zipper closed again, setting some sort of speed record for the action.

Golly released him suddenly and I was at the man's side in an instant.

"Dr. Wade," I said. "It's me, Jim Wiley. I'm very sorry for what just happened, but—"

"Just what the devil is going on?" he exclaimed, rising and turning toward me.

Then he saw Golly and he began to back away, edging along the table. He raised his arm and pointed.

"That man attacked me!" he announced.

"Yes, sir. He's a security guard," I said. "We had a problem here earlier, and he was sent over to keep an eye on things."

"But I told him I'm a member of the foundation, that I have identification in my wallet. He paid no attention whatso—"

"He doesn't understand English," I said, truthfully. "He was the best we could get on short notice."

"You should have done something," he said, "to prevent authorized people from being assaulted."

"We did," I answered, not realizing till after I said it that it might be taken as an impertinence. "We hung out the Closed sign."

"Not on the back door, you didn't," he stated, "and that's the one my key fits. If any other members were to show up that's the way they'd come in, too."

"I'm sorry," I said again. "You're right, of course. I'll post a notice there as soon as I go downstairs. It's my fault. I should have thought of that. It never even occurred to me that anyone might come by at this hour."

He adjusted his glasses and ran a hand through his wiry gray and brown hair. He was a tall, lanky man, a mathematician who worked at the lab up in Los Alamos. He was also the head of one of the foundation-sponsored projects, and he did indeed have every right to be here any time he chose, should he need to go through the project files or something related.

"What sort of problem did you have earlier?" he asked, his voice suddenly milder.

"Someone tried to break in," I said. "It seems he got frightened off, though."

He glanced past me at Barry, who was standing quietly beside the door.

"Why are you boys over here, then?" he wanted to know.

"My father got called away suddenly earlier in the evening," I explained. "I'm sure he would have thought to put the sign up out back."

"I trust he'll be back soon," Dr. Wade said.

"I really hope so," I replied.

"His absence is related to this—security matter?"

"Oh yes. Very much so," I answered.

He smoothed his shirtfront and began picking up some scattered papers and placing them into a manila folder, from which they had fallen.

"Well, you seem to have done the right thing in calling a security person and closing the place down," he said, "though it was probably only your standard urban prowler, and I'm sure he's long gone. Look, I drove all the way down from the Hill because I only had my personal notes on a meeting we'd had last week, and I wanted to go over the whole file."

He tapped the folder with his forefinger.

"I was planning on taking one of the bedrooms upstairs," he went on, "and staying over after I'd reviewed this stuff. I'm willing to take my chances. I doubt that whoever it was will come back, now you've been alerted. And even if he does"—he glanced at Golly and smiled—"I'd feel perfectly safe."

What could I say? I didn't like it, but I felt outranked.

"I guess that's your decision to make," I began, "but—"

"Good," he said, squeezing my shoulder. "It's a fair drive back, and falling asleep at the wheel is probably a bigger danger than anything going on down here."

"Would you like us to make you a pot of coffee?"

"No, thanks. I brought a thermos."

I noticed as he glanced that way that an

overnight bag rested on the chair beside the door.

"Funny," he said, crossing the room and picking up the bag. "There seems to be stuff about this meeting that I don't remember." He waved the folder. "I must have been dozing when someone circulated the equations."

"Equations?" I said.

"Yes, there's a whole sheet of them I don't recall at all. Kind of fascinating, too. I'm looking forward to going over them. Good night, Jim. You too, Barry."

He headed out the doorway and left us standing there with our Golem and a feeling that things had somehow gotten even stranger.

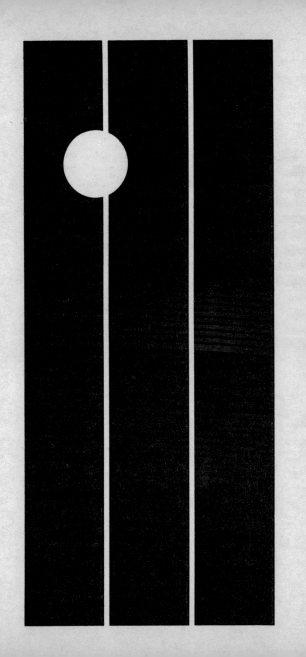

IV

We made another sign there in the library, and we put it up on the back door when we went downstairs. We set Golly to continue his patrolling, since we knew he wouldn't bother Dr. Wade anymore. We also made sure that the mathematician was well settled in his room upstairs and, hopefully, unlikely to wander. When these things were done we returned next door to our kitchen, where Becky still waited.

The first thing that Barry said to me when we were back in our own quarters was, "Are you sure that's really Dr. Wade?"

"Yes," I answered. "I am."

"Some of those darkbanders are shapeshifters, you know."

"I know," I said, "and he's not one of them. They can't shift their smell. I know his. Also, the strange smell that was there earlier is just about gone now."

"It's safe to go over, then?" Becky asked.

"I'm sure of it."

"So what do we do now?" Barry asked.

"We all go back to the transcomp room."

"Why?"

"There's something I want to see—a clue I missed, I think."

"What kind of clue?" Becky wanted to know.

I turned and left the kitchen with both of them following.

"The more I think of it, the more I'm certain that Dad escaped through the transit field," I said. "Whoever he'd been fighting with didn't. That's why I smelled him all over the place earlier. But he's gone now too."

"So?" Barry asked. "We don't know where they went and we're stuck with a broken machine."

"One thing at a time," I said as we passed back into the foundation hallway. "The most important thing right now is to figure out where Dad went."

Barry nodded.

"And if he did transit out, we ought to be able to tell where he is from the band setting."

"Yeah," Barry agreed quickly. "You may be right . . ." He paused a moment and then added, "But what if the other guy changed the setting afterward to confuse us?"

"Why should he have?" I answered. "If he broke the machine and we can't use it, it doesn't matter. Besides, I get the impression he was in a hurry."

We entered the storeroom, turned on the light, and advanced to the panel. In a moment I had it open and we were heading down the stairs.

We entered the transcomp room, which was unchanged, and I hurried forward and read the band setting. I found it puzzling, but I pulled the chart from the drawer to confirm what my memory was telling me. In the meantime, Barry had come up and was studying the dial.

"That's a darkband setting," he stated. "The third one, I think."

He was right, and I nodded.

"Yes," I said, "but since our equipment doesn't penetrate there, there has to be another explanation. And I think I see it." I reached out and tapped with my knuckles, hard, above the dial. The indicator dropped. "See?" I said. "It probably jumped when the equipment was struck."

"But is it in a real band right now?" he asked. "Or is it just out of tune?"

I waved the chart.

"This is a dense area," I said. "That's a bona fide band it fell to."

"Which one is it?"

"Well, it's a deadband," I said.

"Hmm."

He reached forward and recalibrated the tuner to the original setting. Abruptly he struck the chassis beneath the dial. This time the needle jogged upward.

"Anything there?" he asked.

"Yes. A lightband."

"Hmm."

"I see what you mean," I said. "It could have jumped to the darkband from above or below."

"Exactly," he replied. "Are there any others adjacent to these?"

"No."

"I didn't think so. I thought I remembered that cluster."

Becky came forward and studied the chart.

"I've visited both of those bands," Barry said. "You have, too, of course."

"No," I replied. "Only the deadband."

"I thought you'd been to all of the light-bands."

"All but one," I said, "and that's the one."

"How come you didn't go there?"

"Well, that's where my Uncle George lives."

"So?"

"He's a shapeshifter, and I seem to take after him. Something about that place is particularly conducive to the phenomenon. He'd cautioned my folks not to bring me there until I was older and could gain conscious control of the process. Otherwise there was the possibility I might turn into a wolf and run off into the wilds."

"So that's what this full moon business has been about with you?"

"Yep."

He drummed his fingers on the tabletop for a moment, then said, "And that might very well be the band he'd flee to, if he has a brother there."

"Brother-in-law," I corrected. "It's Mom's folks. But yes, you're right. That could be it."

"On the other hand," Becky said suddenly, "a deadband could be a very good hiding place."

"There is that," I said. "But why?"

"Why what?"

"Why hide? All he really had to do was get away. They obviously wanted to penetrate here, and they succeeded. There's nothing really personal about something like that. He just happened to be in the way. They wouldn't be chasing after him now. They'd be about the business they'd come to take care of."

"I wonder . . ." she said.

"What?"

"Whether there might not be more to it than that," she finished.

"Why should there be?"

"Just a feeling I have," she said. "Just a funny feeling."

I shrugged. Nobody ever tells me anything.

"Your feeling doesn't matter if we can't go after him," Barry said. "And if we could, it still doesn't matter. He's safe from the dark-banders now—if they really came after him personally."

She pointed at the dial.

"A darkbander could have looked at that and come to the same conclusion you did," she said.

He chewed his lower lip for a moment.

"Okay, you've got a point," he said then. "There *might* be darkband agents after him, and we should be careful if we follow him. I don't think that's really the case, but it's better to be safe. Of course, all of this is academic," he finished, "if we can't transit out. Have you ever worked on the equipment, Jim?"

"Some," I said. "Pretty standard maintenance stuff. But Dad always had me watch when he did any kind of real work on it, and he explained things as he went along."

"It was the same with me back home," he acknowledged. "I guess we'd better check it out."

I flipped on the power and showed him the one lit indicator.

"We could still probably receive," I said. "The damage is in transmission."

"That doesn't do us any good."

I killed the power again and unscrewed the damaged panel. When I pried it off he stared and shook his head.

"Uh-oh," he said.

"Yeah."

"There's a lot of work there. . . ."

"How long will it take to fix it?" Becky asked.

"We're going to be working on it all night," Barry said, "even if we just replace everything."

"Do you *have* replacements for everything?" she asked.

"I'm not sure," I answered.

"If we've got to try repairing some of the parts as well, it's going to take a lot longer."

"You're right," I agreed. "Then we're going to have to pull a lot of checks on it."

"Has either of you ever done a job like that?" Becky asked.

"Not me," I said.

Barry shook his head.

"Then it's too long and too uncertain," she told us.

Barry laughed, without humor.

"If you've got a better idea, let us know," he said.

"There might be another way for you to transit," she said.

"Don't be silly," Barry responded. "Either you've got a functioning transcomp or you don't."

She gave him a long, hard stare. Finally, he looked away.

"Well, what do you know that we don't?" he said then.

She smiled, for the first time in a long while.

"That's the wrong question," she told him, "when time is so important. Supposing there is another way of getting you to those worlds? How would you go about finding Tom?"

"In the case of the lightband," Barry said, "we just ask the people on that side—the

Kendalls—where he is. After all, he'd have come through on their equipment. For the deadband there'll be no people to ask, of course. But he'd be in the hidden station, or near it. You know that. You've been to those places yourself and—"

"That's not what I mean," she said. "If this works, I'm not at all sure you'll arrive near the other transcomps. Probably not. I want to know whether you know your way well enough to get there on your own if I can transit you to the general vicinity."

Barry studied her, his eyes narrowing.

"You're serious, aren't you?" he asked. Then, seeing her expression at that, he continued hurriedly, "Well, yes. I think so. I mean, that's one of the reasons for all of the visiting we've done back and forth over the years, and for all the studying about each other's worlds, all the maps and histories. So we can find our way around in them if we have to. If you know a way of getting us there I think we could locate the proper places."

He glanced at me and I nodded.

"I've no idea what you have in mind," I said to her. "But if you can send us, can you also bring us back?"

"No. I'd have to be there," she said. "I'll lose track of you once you're gone. But you said our transcomp can still receive. So turn it on, set it, leave it on, and have the people at that station send you back when you're ready."

"We'd have to be sure that it *really* receives," I said. "Just because a light goes on and we get a humming sound doesn't mean everything's just right."

She shrugged.

"That's your department," she said. "Find out."

"You're right," I agreed, "and we will. But even so, I don't see how you can send us."

She looked away.

"I don't *know* that I can," she said. "All I can do is try. It's the Old Way."

"What do you mean?"

"How did they manage the transits before they had computers?" she asked.

"The computer isn't absolutely necessary. It just makes things a lot easier," I said. "In the old days you had to do a lot more pencil-and-paper work and manual adjustments for band drift and stuff like that."

"That's not the old days," she said. "I mean the *real* old days. What did they do back before they could just push a plug into the wall and throw a switch?"

"They set up their own private power sources," I said. "Windmills, running water. Stuff like that. They learned the tricks from the more technologically advanced bands."

"Uh-huh," she said. "How'd they get in touch with them to learn that stuff?"

"It must have been the other way around. They got in touch with us."

"Just tuned in on our nonexistent machinery, huh?"

"Well, I'm not sure exactly how they reached the Founder and told him what to build—"

"You don't know."

"No, I don't know."

"There are other power sources than windmills and running water," she said. "We are going to do it the way it was done in the days before the Founder. The Old Way."

Barry was staring at her, wide-eyed, the fingers of his right hand tracing a strange design in the air. Becky ignored this entirely.

"So you guys check out the receiver," she said, "while I go and get some things together."

She turned and left the room.

"She really *is* a witch!" Barry said softly.

I shrugged. I already knew that.

V

As we checked over the machine I thought of the various bands and of what we all meant to each other. There are several bands about equivalent to ours technologically—ahead of us in a few ways, behind in a few others, on a par in most. Then there are a few that are definitely in advance of ours in most ways. Others are behind us, at various levels ranging from feudal through early industrial stages. The families study all of the time lines like mad, hoping to learn from mistakes in each other's development, trying to foresee the periodic crises through which every culture seems to pass, doing our best to make these transitions as smooth as possible.

Our commerce is mainly one of ideas, and our office has not always been located in the American Southwest. We have moved about from generation to generation, setting up in those centers where our influence will work the most benefit. After numerous family conferences, our ancestors in London actually brought in an associate from a high-tech band, coached him, and sent him to Dublin in the early nineteenth century. There he engaged in numerous drinking bouts with a troubled mathematician named Hamilton, with occasional talk of the symbolization of vectors in three-dimensional space. Years later Hamilton's work was ready and waiting when Heisenberg had need of it. It was rough on our associate's liver but proved useful in helping to understand the atomic age when it became necessary to do so.

Right now we run a foundation near Los Alamos, and some of the people from the lab, like Dr. Wade, are members. It is a genuine think tank, which accepts legitimate contracts on which our members can earn extra money by brainstorming ideas into reports and recommendations. And every now and then they may get fed an outside idea, something not always applicable to the problem at hand but which may well be recalled in another context, somewhere down the line.

All of this, of course, must be done very carefully and after considerable deliberation, in light of our knowledge of all of our histories. For the wrong idea at the wrong time can be as dangerous as the right one can be useful. And according to family discussions, it seems that our band is passing through some fairly delicate times just now.

All of which makes everything sound very mechanistic and predictable, which by no means is really the case. A couple of the less developed lightbands seem to contain phenomena which do not lend themselves to easy explanation. Stories keep cropping up, for instance, of unusual people and magical-seeming happenings, which are very hard to investigate or explain.

Such as a band Dad and Mom visited about seven years ago. Feudal, agrarian, low tech. Castles, manor houses, nobles, serfs. Like that.

It was being discussed whether improved methods of spinning and weaving wool, which would profoundly affect the economy of a large area there, should be introduced at about that time. (They weren't.)

At the time, their host came down with one of his migraine headaches and said that he wanted to visit an old woman who lived in the neighborhood who had been successful in treating these in the past. She was nominally a midwife and herbalist, but he believed she possessed genuine paranormal abilities of a healing sort. So they rode out to her place. They discovered her to be dead when they got there, and foul play was involved, though nothing more was ever learned as to motives or guilty parties. But something more was discovered: a little girl was found hiding, crying, in the woods nearby. She called the old woman Granny, and neighbors told them that she'd lived with her for some time, though no one seemed to know whether they were actually related. And none of them knew of any other relatives of the girl's. Her name was Becky, and she hung on to my mother and cried. That's how I acquired a sister.

Becky doesn't talk to me about her early memories. But then, nobody believes in telling me anything important around here. Maybe she told Mom about things from when she was little. I just don't know. They seemed to have developed some sort of special bond early on. Becky's occasionally let something slip, though, and she does peculiar things and she seems to have ways of knowing things she shouldn't really know about.

Tonight was one of those times, with all that

talk about Old Ways and of doing a transit without the machine. Becky does okay in school, but she doesn't really have that many friends. And maybe it isn't all that healthy that she spends all the time she does staring into flames and things like that. I don't know. But that's the sort of thing that made me kind of think of her as a witch. I never really doubted, though, that she had some peculiar secrets, and I'd a funny feeling that whatever she was about to do would be something I couldn't really understand. I shivered suddenly.

"The receiver seems okay," Barry said. "But you know, if we were to go away and leave it on, anybody who knows the proper frequency for our station could come through or send something."

I nodded.

"If it's friends it doesn't matter," I said. "As for the darkbanders, I think they've already come and gone. I suppose we could leave Golly down here, though, to mind the store."

"I think that would be a good idea," he responded. "Do you have any idea what Becky is going to do?"

"No."

I checked over the receiver myself. It seemed that he was right about it.

"Well, I don't know what's going to happen or how long it's going to take," I said. "So I guess I'll go collect Golly and bring him down here to be a watchdog. You stay here, in case she gets back before I do. Okay?"

"Sure," he said, jamming his hands into his pockets when I glanced at them. I'd only glanced at them because of the movement, and it had taken me seconds to realize that they were shaking. And it took me several seconds more to realize why.

Barry came from one of the bands where unusual people and happenings sometimes occur. But it had never occurred to me before that he might be sort of superstitious, or that he could actually be afraid of Becky.

I grinned, hoping to put him somewhat at ease, and I slapped him on the shoulder as I went by.

"Hold the fort," I said, and I hurried on up the stairs.

As I passed through rooms and up more stairs, seeking our silent, stalking Golem, I wondered whether there might actually be some basis for Barry's fears. Becky had seemed fairly sure of herself, reasonably confident about whatever it was that she was going to try. It seemed obvious that she knew something that we didn't know—or thought she did. Where could she have learned it? She had been too small when she had come to live with us to have had much in the way of complicated instruction from the old woman. The only alternative I could think of was that she might have learned some means of self-instruction. On those occasions when she sat in her room meditating, was she in communication with someone—or something—that taught her things of an unusual nature? The sudden thought of something like that going on up the hall from me for all these years was more than a little disturbing. If there were something more involved than Becky's own drifting mind, how was I to know whether it was something good, or—otherwise?

I snorted at this, and then I chuckled. I could see that I was overreacting to a series of guesses, and I knew that it had something to do with how upset I felt over Dad's disappearance. Becky had been my sister for most of my life—hers too, for that matter. She could get pretty mad at me on occasion, but I could never see her doing anything that would really hurt me. She just wasn't the sort to go around curdling milk, making dogs howl, and giving people the Evil Eye. If she did possess any sort of strange knowledge, she'd want to use it to help us. I knew that because I knew what she was like.

She's all right.

I caught a whiff of that faint, new car smell Golly exudes, and I followed it to the small records room up the hall from the library. Sure enough, I found him inside, moving in a slow circuit about the place, checking into every chink and cubby. I approached him, was recognized, opened his control panel, and changed his instructions. I took his hand in mine then and led him out the door.

"This way, Golly," I said. "I've got a new job for you."

Becky had not yet returned when we got back to the transcomp room, but she showed up shortly after I had programmed Golly to guard the place and set him to stand sentry near the door. She came rushing in, a bulging pillowcase in her arms, screamed briefly when she saw Golly, let go, then grabbed at and recovered her bundle.

"I wish you'd let me know you'd brought that thing in here," she said.

"I'm sorry," I told her.

She frowned and moved away from the Golem.

"You could have slowed things down quite a bit if I'd broken any of this stuff," she stated.

"I said I'm sorry."

"Okay. Apology accepted," she said. "Is that receiver turned on?"

"Yes," Barry answered, his back against the wall, his eyes following her every move.

"Good." She cleared a space in the center of the floor by removing a chair, a wastebasket, and a stack of periodicals to the room's far corner. She set the pillowcase in the clear area, knelt, and reached inside. She withdrew a candle and a candle holder, fitted them together, and set them on the floor before her. Then she took out a package of matches, lit the candle, and raised her head. "Would one of you please turn out the lights?" she asked.

Barry nodded, crossed to a position beside the door, and flipped the switch.

"And close the door," she said, "so the light from the passage won't interfere."

He pushed it shut.

Becky rummaged in the pillowcase again and withdrew more candles and more burnished holders. While she was fitting the candles in, she said, "Okay, do you know what you are going to do if I am able to open the way for you to reach those two bands?"

"In the case of the deadband," I said, "I just have to search in the area of the transcomp. It's hidden in the basement of a ruined building. He could be holed up right there. If he isn't, he may have left a message. If there is no message, then a quick search of the area would probably turn up some sign if he'd been by. If I find any such indication I'll try following it. If I don't I'll come back, and we can scratch that one."

"Same idea here," Barry said. "Only easier,

since there'll be people around to ask. I'll just
go through and check with the Kendalls as to
whether he transitted in on their equipment. If
he did, he'll probably still be there with them."

Becky pursed her lips and studied the flame
as she slowly raised another taper and lit it
from the first one. She set it aside and reached
for another.

"No," she said as she did this. "It won't be
quite that easy. As I said, I should be able to
get you into the general vicinity of the stations, but I don't think that I can bring you in
right on target. So you have to be ready to find
your own ways from wherever you might arrive."

She lit another taper. Their flickering light
upon her face made her look stranger, older.

"How far?" Barry asked. "I'd be in trouble if
you set me on another continent or something
like that."

"No. Nothing like that," she said. "But I
could be off twenty or thirty miles or so, something on that order. You'd still be in the general area."

"I can manage that," Barry answered. "I spent
over a month there once. I know the neighborhood."

I thought back over street maps I had memo-
rized of the ruined city, over various topograph-
ical features I had had to learn, as well as the
different places I could head to orient myself.

"I'll be okay," I said.

She continued to light candles, lining them
up to her left. Shadows danced upon the walls
now, and across the surfaces of the equipment.
Golly looked positively sinister in the gloom,
like some figure in a wax museum. Even the
faint drone of the transit receiver, hardly no-

ticeable before, now seemed like the sound track
of some film right before disaster hits.

"Okay, then," she said. "Gather round." And
she motioned us to sit in positions on the floor
so that we formed a triangle, facing inward.

She withdrew three vanity mirrors from the
pillowcase and set them up along the sides of
the triangle, between us, so that each of us
faced one mirror. Then she began placing the
candles in a kind of zigzag array in the middle.
There were seven of them, and we each faced
their glowing reflections as well as the things
themselves. The room suddenly seemed cooler,
despite the small heat from the flames.

"Uh, anything special we're supposed to do?"
I asked.

"Just watch everything that I do," she said
softly, "and when I tell you to do something
later, just do it. It won't be anything hard."

She reached back into the bundle and there
followed a rattling, clicking sound. She withdrew a handful of brass rods. She placed these
before her on the floor and then took out a pair
of toothed wheels, apparently of the same material. They looked rather like fat, carefully
sculpted gears, save that they were too wide
and the teeth too small for them to have func-
tioned in any sort of machine that I could think
of.

Humming to herself, Becky began laying the
rods among the candles in a different sort of
pattern. There were nine rods, ranging in length
from four to ten inches, about as thick around
as pencils and engraved with serpentine pat-
terns at each end. She set them in place very
slowly, and she switched from humming to sing-

ing as she did so. Her voice remained too low, however, for me to distinguish any words.

I watched her hands as they moved among the flames. I watched the light sliding along the lengths of the rods as she adjusted them. I also watched the reflections across the way of her hands and the lights and the rods. Her low tuneless tune filled my mind.

She picked up one of the wheels in each hand, fit them together, and turned them very slowly by pressing upon them and sliding her hands in opposite directions. Then back, then apart again. Back and apart. They made a gentle clicking sound in accompaniment to her strange tune. The lights seemed to flow together for a moment into a single bright smear. As this occurred I heard, briefly, a new sound—a high, keening note, almost a whine. It was gone in an instant, but it returned when the smear came again.

"What's happening?" Barry asked.

Becky glared at him and he shut up.

She continued for what seemed a long while after that, and the periods of brightness came closer and closer together. Finally, she set the two wheels, still touching, on the ground before her, and with her right hand she continued to roll them back and forth. With her left she began moving the rods into a new position.

Then, "Barry," she said, "stand up," and from the corner of my eye I saw him do it.

"Turn around," she went on, "and start walking."

He moved, I heard a few footsteps, then nothing.

I continued to stare into the light, to listen

to the clicking and the keening. There were moments when Becky seemed very far away.

Her left hand moved again, creating a new pattern with the rods. She sang again for a time, and my vision swam and was filled with light.

"Rise now," she said, and her voice was faint, as from a great distance. I did as she directed, and then, "Turn around," she said.

I did an about-face, and the air was filled with dancing motes before me, countless after-images of the light into which I had been staring, blinking and darting like innumerable fireflies.

"Walk," she said, and I did.

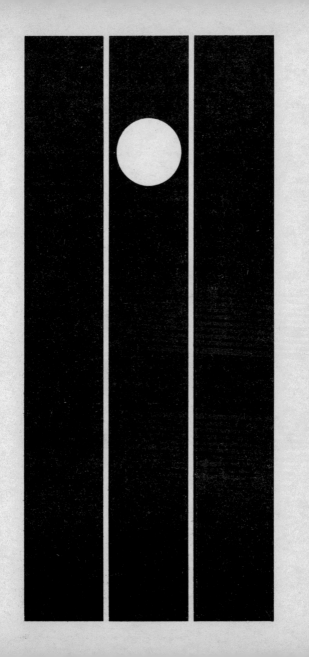

VI

I moved slowly, because I felt I should be running into something very soon. But after a time I realized that I had taken more steps than was possible, moving in a straight line in any direction in that room. Therefore, it would seem I was no longer in the room. And my vision had grown worse instead of better, the darting lights becoming brighter and more numerous—which just isn't the way afterimages usually behave. I noted, too, at about that time that the surface upon which I trod was no longer smooth. Therefore, it wasn't the floor.

Ahead of me was one big bright sheet of light, and I seemed to be advancing upon it. My feet and my hands tingled somewhat, and the entire experience was somehow not an unfamiliar one.

I still seemed to hear Becky singing, faintly, and I realized that it was important I keep moving, that I not halt until I reached the light or stopped hearing her voice. My feelings were a bit disconcerting, as if I were somehow stuck at a point halfway between sleep and waking. I realized then that I had no idea how long I had been walking.

I realized something else, too, and I knew why the experience seemed familiar. All of the sensations I was feeling were a protracted version of the momentary tingling, swirling, flash-flecked sensation I'd known when doing a cross-over by means of the transcomp.

So I kept walking and the light kept growing, and the only comforting thing about the whole business was Becky's fading tune. Soon the light came to dominate my field of vision. Then it seemed to grow even more rapidly, out of pace with my approach, until I felt that it was rushing toward me and then realized moments later that this was indeed the case—

In one bright, frightening instant I passed through, and everything was changed.

I kept moving, automatically, discovering myself to be passing along a dirt trail, shadow-decked trees at either hand. All of the light now present had resolved itself into a sky full of stars and a larger glow somewhere off to my right, its source masked by dark boughs. There was a faint rustling of leaves and branches stirred by cool breezes. I heard the occasional cries and stridencies of birds and insects. The smells of damp soil, leaf mold, and fresh growing things came to me strongly; also, there were the scents of a number of animals, some of them familiar, some not so, against a hint of distant fresh water.

This was all wrong. I had expected nuclear winter, damaged buildings, rusting vehicles, dust, broken glass; in short, decades-old carnage. Instead, I found myself walking a quiet trail through an uncontaminated countryside. While this was certainly a more congenial place than the other, it was of no help to us whatsoever. It was wrong. Becky had somehow messed up. It—

No.

As I passed along the trail, and the treeline to my right dipped and retreated, I saw that the larger light from that direction came from the bright face of a full moon. Immediately, my hands began itching despite the cool breezes, and I felt perspiration break out upon my forehead. A jittery restlessness came over me, followed by a sudden shortness of breath, though I was not exerting myself particularly. And I knew then what had happened.

I had a mental image of Barry walking the broken streets of a blasted, deserted city. Obviously, Becky had sent Barry to the deadband rather than me, while I had been transported to the band I was supposed to avoid until I was older and, hopefully, better able to gain control of the process that even now seemed to be commencing. Not only had I been sent to the wrong place, I had arrived at the worst possible time.

I halted, panting, and raised my hands to my face. I could feel the stubble again in the places I had shaved earlier. I was suddenly aware of cramps in my legs, beginning in my calves and spreading up into the muscles of my thigh shortly thereafter. As I leaned over to massage them I felt pains in my shoulders.

I seemed to be cross-eyed, for my nose suddenly seemed longer and darker by moonlight. There came an audible creaking from my joints and a series of sharp lower back pains.

I tried to recall everything I knew about the phenomenon. For those of us who are susceptible to the change, there are supposed to be ways of resisting it and, ultimately, ways of controlling it. Unfortunately, I lacked particu-

lars, having also been told that one had to
experience the things first in order to realize
how any controlling techniques applied. Great.
I had hardly set out with a rite of passage in
mind, but it looked as if my education was
about to be furthered. It promised to be an
interesting night.

I decided to try relaxing, going along with it,
noting all of my reactions as well as I could for
future reference.

Whether rubbing my legs helped them or
whether the cramps went away by themselves,
I do not know. I tried to straighten then, however, and discovered that I was unable to. It
was as if I'd developed a permanent crick in
my back. At least there was no pain associated
with this. Realizing what was going on, though,
I clawed hurriedly at my belt, noting that my
hands seemed smaller and hairier, the fingers
shorter. If I were going to transform I wanted
to get undressed in a hurry. I did not want to
find myself a big, doglike creature helplessly
entangled in jeans, T-shirt, and tennis shoes.

I had to lie on my side to finish the job, and
a steady series of aches rippled through my
body as I thrashed about on the ground. My
feet came out of my shoes looking suspiciously
pawlike, and I'd a funny feeling I was developing something I could wag on my rear end.
This could become extremely awkward, I realized, if I were separated from my garments
when I retransformed, especially if there were
ladies in the vicinity. I tried gathering my
clothes up, with some idea of making a bundle
of them that I could carry about in my mouth.
But it was too late; my hands were no longer
hands, and when I picked the loose garments

up in my teeth I could see that they'd just drag and snag on things.

But I actually was trying to relax the entire time, to feel what each twinge did to me, as the fevers and chills alternated, my muscles spasmed, my bones seemed to shift about. There were times when it almost seemed I might be able to exert some control over the process, but I didn't dare. The last thing I needed was to mess things up and wind up some kind of freak. A crippled werewolf struck me as a pretty pathetic creature. So I just lay there and felt it and let it run its course. The one time I yelled, during a particularly painful twisting, it came out as a howl. Something in the genes, of course. I told myself that it had to be genetic.

Still, such considerations became more and more academic as the process continued. I knew that it affected my mind, though I could not have provided details at the time on everything that it did to my thinking. It seemed that my sense of the passage of time was somehow altered, though, for when the change had run its course I felt that the moon was higher in the heavens than it should be for the amount of time that seemed to have gone by. I didn't believe that this was just a matter of position, with me standing on all fours now—though my vision was no longer as good as it had been. On the other hand—or maybe I should say "paw" —my hearing was enormously enhanced. Every tiny creak or rustle produced by the wind in its passage through the foliage, every little bug whistle, claw scrape, wing rustle, and fall of footpad came to me in full-fidelity stereo, some of the sounds almost painful. And my sense of smell, as highly developed as it was, had never been this good before. I knew from a few whiffs of the air exactly where the stream was located; I could tell where a rabbit had fled a little while ago, knew there was a fox in the vicinity, retreating now.

I took a slow step forward. Then another. It felt funny. I walked again, and I started thinking about my movements and I stumbled. I stood and tried again. I stumbled again. Frustrated, I raised my muzzle and howled. The sound frightened me a bit, as I hadn't planned on doing it. It just came out. But it made me realize that if I could howl without thinking I could probably walk without thinking, too—in fact, I might be better off not thinking about such things at all for now, and relying on reflex and instinct without letting my mind get in the way.

So I tried again with my mental machinery idling and this time I walked just fine. But there was more to come, and it was frightening. Apparently, the change was still going on, and not necessarily at a purely physical level. For when I put my thinking in abeyance and let my newly formed body take over, strange thoughts began to flit through my mind. They were not the sort of thoughts I had ever thought before. They were . . . hunting thoughts.

My head would drop low and move from side to side, and I would sniff the ground, seeking trails. Whenever I discovered one I realized that I knew what had passed there and how long ago the passing had occurred. Then I would raise my head high and sniff the breezes, seeking more distant scents. I passed among trees as I did these things, and images of fleeing game, myself pursuing it, passed through my mind. A part of me realized that I had had some destination in mind earlier. But that part, which I had put to rest to keep from stumbling, now seemed a very small part indeed. It was overwhelmed, more than half buried. Its objective was no longer of first importance. It would have to wait on the hunt.

It seemed as if a part of me were going to sleep, while another part, one I had not ever realized to be present, was waking up. To the drowsing me, everything that followed seemed somehow like a dream. I came later to wonder whether the me I had always been was like a dream to that sleeping other. . . .

Dreaming.

Running at a steady lope, the night alive with sounds and scents. Down hillside, along stream's dark bank. Pausing to drink the cold black water. All shapes are gray. The earth is signed with the smell of smaller game. I take a trail, follow for a time, lose it, try another. Moving quickly now, shadow amid shadows. Slipping ghostlike through brush and bramble. My senses extend me beyond my skull. I am become a piece of the night.

It is hunger, the rush of events, the heat of the hunt. Ahead, I hear movements. It knows I am coming. It flees. I taste the darkness, I hear the song the moon sings. . . .

There is no time, and as for space, it seems I move with such ease that the world rushes to meet me. I am suspended in the dark dream of the hunt, where reason sleeps as the scroll of sensation unwinds. I am dog-shaped death within the wood of the world, thing of fang and hunger. Beneath sky's eyes beast to feast blooding moon-turned hours . . .

I was lost within the bitter dream of predator and prey, time without time, as night washed me and carried me far away. I know that I caught and I killed, and I ate, small furred things which sometimes squealed, but beyond this my waking consciousness censored much of the detail. I remember that at the time it had seemed the right thing to do—more than right, actually.

There was one point, well into the night's hunting, when my exuberance rose into a long, drawn out howl. Almost immediately, from across a great distance, I was answered by a similar voice. This reply drew me up short for a moment with a sort of tingling reaction I did not fully understand. The call was not repeated, however, and I was back on the track a short while later.

There are blurred spots and missing areas to that night, as there are in any dream or in any day of steady, repetitious activity. There were times when I slowed, times when I rested, times when I drank again from pool or stream. It seems that I was always alert, however, and that I still hunted with my mind even when my body was resting or otherwise engaged. Then, somewhere toward dawn, I began to tire, to slow. There were new scents in the air then, as of human habitation, but these were still sufficiently removed that I was not apprehensive.

I rested in a glade, tongue lolling, sides heaving, ears pricked and mobile. Had I been capable of speech at that time I would have said that nothing could have approached without my becoming aware of its presence. Just shows how wrong you can be. One night out does not give a novice werewolf a graduate degree in woodlore.

It had approached my resting place from downwind, with absolute silence. It would have been difficult to believe that anything that large could move with such stealth against a hyper-sensitive creature such as I had become, save for my own recent experience. I remember that the grasses had grown moist and that the faintest spillage of dawn had begun in one corner of the sky when I received the first indication that I was not alone.

There came a single soft footfall from somewhere to my rear, and I was on my feet and turning even as I heard a low growled sound that seemed strangely like a word—my name. I beheld a wolf even larger than the one I had become, gray, and with large glinting yellow eyes. Flight would be useless, I decided, for I knew that it would catch me and have me at a disadvantage for my having fled, taking me from the rear. Fighting did not seem such a great idea either, but better here while I was rested than somewhere else when I was winded. There seemed no alternative, for why else would it have stalked me if not to do me harm?

With a snarl, I launched myself at the intruder, going for the throat with my teeth. But it turned quickly, its shoulder striking my shoulder, knocking me to the ground. In an instant, I felt teeth upon my throat—but they did not tighten. From my drowsing mind flashed a memory of something I had read concerning dominance and submission among wolves, that whole business about the loser exposing his throat to the victor, who then was bound to go no further with the attack. So I lay still. At some other level, also, it seemed the best thing to do. I just hoped this wolf had read the same book.

I lay there without moving, and the other's fangs exerted but the barest pressure upon my neck. This went on for what seemed a long while, and then the pressure was gone, the muzzle withdrawn. A growling followed, modulated so that it sounded like *"James."*

I stared, for the wolf began doing some very unwolflike things. It reared several times upon its hind legs, front paws extended high into the air. Then it commenced rolling about the ground, legs splayed at various odd angles. I realized what was going on moments later as its appearance grew more and more manlike, and even familiar. . . .

I tried growling and forming words within it, as he had done. I tried saying "Uncle George!" though I couldn't be sure how it sounded to him. He did smile, though, as he nodded at me.

"I can see where you'll be needing some lessons in this business," he said. "We'll start with one of the quick ways of changing back."

I nodded my muzzle. It's always good to have an expert in the family.

VII

When I finished retransforming I realized that I was cold and very, very tired.

"Come on," Uncle George said, taking hold of my arm. "I've a cart not too far from here. We'll ride back to the manor."

I followed him among the trees.

"I hope you brought a blanket or something," I said, my teeth beginning to chatter. "I don't feel too good."

"I know all about it, boy, and I brought warm clothes for you."

I found myself panting and I leaned on him as we walked, my feet grown wet from dew. When I stopped panting I began yawning, one after another. I couldn't stop.

"Oxygen," he said as we trekked through the wood. "You need a lot. It's partly because I hurried things to get you through the change fast. Even without hurrying it can be fatiguing."

"You don't seem tired," I managed.

"I know what I'm doing," he told me. "I can control it."

"You've got to teach me more about it."

"All in good time," he said.

When we reached his cart, where a gentle-looking brown mare eyed us and snorted once, softly, from her position between the traces, I had to lean against the cart's side to stay standing while I drew on the trousers and the loose-fitting shirt Uncle George passed me. I stood wrapped in a dark blue cloak he had passed me, almost in a daze, while he dressed himself. He gave me a hand up into the cart. I'm not sure I could have made it on my own.

"You knew I'd be here tonight," I managed, as I sprawled on the cart's bed and drew the cloak about me.

"Yep," he said, as he took hold of the reins and shook them gently.

We moved forward, and I did not get to voice the rest of my questions because my mind fuzzed over and drifted, and talking was too much trouble. So was thinking. I felt myself going away. I slept.

I dreamed a bit—strange, disorganized things. There's a guy I know who got a summer job as a bank teller. He told me that after he'd been at it for a while, he began having "teller dreams," dreams of standing there at the window counting out money interminably. I guess any new, prolonged experience might impress itself on you that way. Mine was strange, though, because it wasn't all that visual, the way most dreams are. I was back in wolf form again, running through the woods, but seeing hadn't been all that important to me then and it wasn't now; my dreams were rushing sequences of smells and sounds, with me looking for something within them, and anything that I did see was mostly at a low angle and close up—roots, grasses, stones, the earth. Then a familiar scent came to me, and I realized that that was what I hunted, even though I did not really know what it represented, except . . .

moving, moving. Blurred images. Scent-path grown stronger. And then I knew. I had entered a clearing and she was there, secured somehow to a tree. My mother . . .

I woke up crying softly, wiping my eyes as the dream faded. Then I drifted back to sleep. This time there were no dreams that I could remember.

I became aware by degrees of the rattling of the cart, the plodding of the mare. For a long while I seemed to drift in that place halfway between sleep and wakefulness. Then I realized that I was no longer cold, and I opened my eyes and there was sunlight all about me. From the sun's position I guessed that I might have slept for a couple of hours. I saw, too, that we were on a much better road now than the rutted forest trail where we had started earlier. The trees had thinned out and were smaller at either hand. We seemed to have come to a higher elevation, also, because when I sat up, facing the rear, I was looking back and down over a great forested area. The shadows of a few drifting clouds to the east moved like dark islands across the bright, leaf green sea contoured of treetop, shrub, and glade. I turned around and saw that we were approaching a large manor house of stone and timber set upon a hilltop, surrounded by a stone wall. Our road led to its front gate. The gate was closed.

"We're almost home," Uncle George said, not looking back. "Thirsty?"

I realized that I was, as he passed me a water bottle without waiting for my answer. I took a long drink, replaced the top, and handed it back.

"Thanks," I said, and I studied our destination. As we drew nearer I heard a low murmuring sound, as of many voices.

I moved into a more comfortable position and checked myself over. My various aches and pains seemed to have vanished as I slept. Most of my fatigue seemed to have washed away also, and what remained seemed to be ebbing rapidly. I was surprised to discover that I was feeling fairly good.

When we finally came up to the gate Uncle George waved to two armed men, who opened it for us.

"Morning," he said. "Any word yet?"

"No," the one on the left replied, "but no trouble either."

"Good."

We rolled inside, and I beheld an armed camp. What had obviously recently been a large, parklike lawn was now well trampled, and there were men spread all over the place, many of them cleaning weapons, helmets, and chest and arm protectors. Cook fires burned here and there, and I could smell rich stews and strong teas. Off to the right, another group of men was eating; to the left, yet another group was being drilled in sword attacks. The three groups seemed to be of about equal size.

"Expecting trouble?" I asked.

"Yes and no," he replied in his typical ambiguous fashion. Uncle George, on those occasions when he had come to visit us, had always been fairly quiet, and when he did talk I was not always certain what he'd said. But I also knew that he could make himself clear when he wanted to. Therefore, now just wasn't one of those times.

He turned onto a small cart trail, which led

us to the rear of the manor. He drew rein before a stable, stepped down, and turned the cart over to a groom, who had emerged when he'd heard us coming. I jumped down from the rear and followed as he headed for a flagged walkway leading beneath some massive elms toward the rear of the house.

"Hungry?" he asked as we entered.

I nodded. Actually, I was more than just hungry. I felt half starved.

"Me, too," he said. "I'll show you to a room where you can clean up while the cook finds us a meal. We'll meet in that side room with the big table," he said, gesturing toward an open doorway to the right, "in a bit."

The room to which he conducted me was about the size of my room back home, though less cluttered. I opened the shutters and a cool breeze came in, along with a view of more ancient trees and a pair of outbuildings. After he had left, I filled a basin with water, pulled off my shirt, and began washing. I realized quickly that I needed it, so I undressed fully and gave myself a sponge bath. I decided on a shampoo also. Several basins and a good towelling later, I opened an armoire and located some fresh garments where Uncle George had told me they would be.

After I'd brushed my hair and rinsed my mouth and cleaned my nails, I departed the room and made my way back to the little room off the kitchen. As I approached it I heard familiar voices. One of them was Aunt Maryl's. The other—

"Barry!" I said as I entered.

He rose from the table, smiling faintly.

"I heard that it happened to you," he said.

I nodded.

"You look okay," he added.

"So do you," I said, and he smiled crookedly.

After I had embraced Aunt Maryl, a tall, dark-haired lady with a small scar above her left eyebrow, I seated myself and filled my plate. Then I glanced at everyone in turn. Barry lowered his fork and said, "I got in last night. When I found myself walking through a wrecked city I realized that Becky must have gotten her signals crossed. It was dark, and it took me a while to figure out that I was across town from the place where the transcomp was hidden. Then it took me a couple of hours more to locate the station."

"And?" I said. "Was Dad . . . ?"

He shook his head.

"No sign at all that he'd been there," he stated. "I struck a light when I unlocked the bunker, and I saw that a fresh layer of dust had settled since the last time I'd been by. My footprints were the only ones, and there were no other indications of anyone's disturbing the place recently. So I set the comp and came through here to let them know you were somewhere in the area."

Uncle George nodded.

"It was easy to figure what happened," he said. "Also, it made it easy for me to find you, if she'd sent you as near to us as she'd sent Barry to that center."

"All right," I said, "I see. And if Dad didn't go through to the deadband that means he came here. Right? Is he okay?"

Uncle George looked away. After a few moments, Aunt Maryl shook her head.

"I'm afraid he didn't come here," she said.

"What do you mean?" I asked. "We figured the possible settings. It had to be that band or this one."

"Well, no," Barry said. "The original setting seems to have been the right one."

I frowned.

"I don't understand," I said. "It was set on a darkband, and they're blocked. You can't get through to them."

He looked at Aunt Maryl.

"Actually, that is not entirely true," she stated. "With the proper tuning one can reach one of the bandit transcomps."

"Bandit transcomps?" I said. "I don't know what you're talking about."

"Your food's getting cold," Uncle George observed.

"I'm not hungry."

"Yes, you are," he said. "Eat, and we'll explain things a bit."

I began eating and my hunger took over. I kept going while they talked.

"The darkband your father transitted to was the third darkband," Aunt Maryl began. "It was formerly a lightband, but it had been successfully invaded several years ago."

I nodded. I already knew this.

"But it was not completely conquered," she continued. "There was a resistance movement. The partisans have their own transcomps, and we've remained in communication with them. The lightbands have been supplying them with strategic materials and personnel since shortly after the conquest."

"Dad knew about this?" I asked.

"Yes. He had been liaison with one such group for a long while. We believe that the darkbanders finally succeeded in tracing his signal. Obtaining the specific frequencies for the various lightband stations has been a top priority of theirs for years. They do have bandit stations of their own in all of the lightbands, but access to a station itself, which is also a field office, would give them the means for more subtle mischief than they could manage otherwise."

"You've lost me," I said.

"They've been trying to pick up your code for a long time," she explained, "and they finally succeeded. It sounds as if Tom fought with whoever came through and escaped by transitting to the bandit station in the darkband—"

"So if you know the frequency we can reach him from here," I said.

"Not so simple," she answered. "They would have silenced their unit and changed its settings almost immediately after Tom got there and told them what had happened. We're sure that's what occurred, because we've tried reaching them and we can no longer pick them up with the old setting."

"That could mean they're all dead and the equipment wrecked!" I said. "The darkbanders must have learned the partisans' code in order to be able to monitor them and pick up Dad's signal. After they'd sent someone through to take care of him, they probably attacked the partisans and wiped them out."

"No," Uncle George interrupted. "It's not that hard to figure their frequency *range* and still not know the exact setting, if they're mainly receiving and not transmitting, which is normally the case. What they probably did was monitor a spectrum for incoming signals. You see, your station was not the only one that was hit—"

"Wait a minute," I said, putting down my fork. "You're making this sound like some kind of war."

"It is," my aunt said. "There has been underground fighting going on ever since the takeover. All of the lightbands have been supporting the rebel forces from the beginning, but the actual conflict has been confined mainly to that band up until now."

"Why is it suddenly spilling over?" I asked.

"The rebels have been growing steadily stronger," she said. "They're now in control of a number of large areas, which include some important cities and installations. It begins to look as if they might actually succeed in obtaining their objectives. So the first darkband is attempting to cut the links to all of their lightband supporters—and giving us problems of our own, to keep us occupied too."

I studied Barry's face for several long moments. "Did you know about all this stuff?" I asked him.

"Well, yes," he answered.

"How come you never mentioned it to me?"

"I was told not to."

"By whom?"

"My parents. Also your father."

"Why shouldn't you have mentioned it?"

"I don't know. They never told me why I shouldn't talk about it."

I looked back at Aunt Maryl.

"Well?" I asked. "Why not? Why has everyone been keeping a thing like this from me?"

"Finish your lunch," Uncle George said.

"I want to know now!"

"Finish your lunch," he repeated. "We'll talk more later."

I studied all of their faces in turn, and I knew I wouldn't get any more out of them just then. I picked up my fork.

VIII

It seems that I am destined always to be surrounded by secrets—and not to be in on most of them. I came to understand the reason behind some of this at a fairly early age, and I know that my position is hardly unique among the kids in the transit families. We go to school with kids in the towns where we make our homes, and we become good friends with some of them. We deal with other people in the community the same as anybody else. If, when I was very young, I'd known too much about the family's special business, there was the possibility I might have let something slip and created thereby an awkward situation. So I wasn't told too much when I was very young, but of course I knew that there was something a bit unusual going on. Kids always do, even if they don't understand. And this was probably the beginning of my paranoia about secrets.

All my life I seem to have been served up information about family affairs on a need-to-know basis. As I said, I could see the reason for it when I was much younger, but I sometimes wondered whether such treatment had simply become a habit with the families, practiced even in matters where it was not strictly necessary. I can remember conversations between my parents that ended with a quick, whispered "Later" or "When he's not around" as I suddenly put in an appearance, or my mother's "I don't want him to know about it"—one of the last things I ever heard her say—with no doubt at all as to whom the "him" referred. Yes, I resent it when I'm treated as if I have no sense and no feelings. And since I was being treated that way again I resented it again. Obviously, something major was going on, with a small army camped on the Kendall's front lawn. If they were willing to tell me about the darkband resistance and the fact that my father had crossed to one of its strongholds, why not finish the story? Why let the cat halfway out of the bag and stop it there?

We finished eating in silence. If someone had at least given me a reason I could have waited—maybe not patiently, but I would have waited until they were ready to tell me the rest. But nobody said a word till we were finished eating, when Uncle George remarked, "Don't go too far off."

"Okay," I said. "Why not?"

"Just don't."

"I want to take a walk out back."

He nodded.

I stamped out, departed through the rear door, and walked off among the trees. I wanted to be alone, which is what I told Barry when he'd tried to follow me. After a time, I came to a small stream, and I sat in the shade on its bank and tossed stones into the water. Not telling me things had to be more than just a habit. The fact that Barry's folks had told him about the fighting in the darkband, and that Dad had asked him not to tell me about it,

proved that Barry's parents trusted him more
than mine trusted me. If you want someone to
be trustworthy it would seem you should try
trusting him every now and then, to give him
a little practice. I threw the next stone with
considerable force. It struck a standing rock,
bounced off, and hit against the side of a tree
on the opposite bank.

I don't enjoy brooding and feeling sorry for
myself. It's a bad way to spend an afternoon. I
realized that I had felt some of these feelings
and thought some of these thoughts before, but
I had always shrugged them off, because I
thought I understood the reasoning that lay
behind my parents' attitude. But it was more
than Barry's knowing things I didn't. The more
I thought of how close Becky and Mom were,
the more certain I was they shared secrets
about which I knew nothing. Then there was
Dave, off on exchange; I'd bet he knew all
kinds of things I didn't.

I spent hours beside that stream in the small
wood to the rear of the manor house, and nobody
came for me, nobody called after me. Several
times I got up and moved on along its course,
because I'd used up all the stones in my immediate vicinity. The sky grew cloudier as the
day advanced, and I half hoped it would rain
on me to match my mood. But it didn't. The
temperature did drop, though, and the breeze
grew more chill. That was something, anyway.

Later—I don't know exactly how much later
—as I was drawing back my arm to cast another stone, something caught my eye in among
the trees on the other side of the stream. There
was a stirring, and a whiteness where there
had been no whiteness before. It took me a

long stare to realize that a patch of mist had risen to hover between a pair of trees as if it were a curtain hung from their limbs. I didn't realize it had grown that damp, and I looked about for other foggy areas, but there were none that I could see. Peculiar . . . But perhaps it was particularly marshy over there. I watched the mist for a time, but though it was stirred, the breeze did not disperse it. Finally, I shied a stone through it but nothing happened.

At last, intrigued, I got to my feet and looked for a place where I could cross over. I located a series of exposed stones farther downstream, and I made it across there. After I'd climbed the bank and backtracked, I spotted the misty area again. It occurred to me that I was really grasping at straws to look for distraction in some will-o'-the-wispy patch of trapped moisture.

But I moved near and stood staring. It wasn't very big, but it was sufficiently dense to be opaque. I noted that the ground beneath my boots did not seem particularly damp, nor did I smell any odd gases. I extended my hand into it. It felt immediately cooler, though it was not masked from my sight. I waved it around a bit, but the fog did not disperse. I started to draw it back, but it seemed at that moment as if I heard a distant singing, and I froze as I tried to figure whether it was real, and where it was coming from if it were.

It faded and I stepped back, letting my hand fall to my side. Just as I did, though, it seemed another sound was beginning. It stopped the moment I lowered my hand.

I stood puzzled. I was certain now that I'd heard something, something which seemed to have its source directly ahead of me, though far removed. Also, it had sounded vaguely familiar. I remembered then, though, that this was one of the bands where magical goings-on were supposedly more likely to occur. Such being the case, it might be possible that I had stumbled upon something of this sort. If so, was this something good, bad, or neutral? Would I be entering a trap if I stepped inside, or might it be something useful or interesting?

The familiarity of the sound nagged, and that is what decided me. I extended my hand again.

This time I heard the singing more clearly, and it sounded so familiar that—

"Becky!" I called as I moved forward. "Becky! Is that you? Where are you?"

I had entered a twilit place, pale to my right and left, darker straight ahead. I had the impression that the dark area led off for a great distance, rather than just a few feet beyond the trees. I could not make out any particular forms within the shadows. I took another step and called again. This time my own voice sounded strange—muffled, flat.

Then, "Jim?" I heard Becky's voice say. "Is that you, Jim?"

"Yeah," I called back. "What's going on?"

"Where are you?"

"I just stepped into a patch of fog behind Aunt Maryl and Uncle George's place," I answered. "I heard your voice."

"Don't come any farther," she said. "But keep talking."

"What should I talk about?"

"Anything. It doesn't matter. I've lost my way. I was looking for you when I got lost. I must have come close, anyway."

"I think you came close," I said.

"So talk, and I'll try to follow your voice."

So I began telling her all of the things that had been bothering me, just to make noise. I was sure she wasn't paying much attention, because she'd started in singing again. *I* wasn't even paying much attention. I knew it all too well.

Her singing grew louder, and after a time it seemed fairly certain that she was approaching. I kept staring ahead, and in a little while I saw a form coming toward me through the mist. It seemed she was headed off a bit to my left, though, so I held out both hands and said, "Becky! Over here!" She altered her course slightly and a moment later she caught hold of my hands.

"Just back up now," she said, "the way you came."

I did, and after only a couple of steps I emerged into the place where I had stood earlier, facing the fog screen. She followed and threw herself into my arms, and I hugged her. Almost immediately, the fog began to disperse.

"I'm sorry," she said. "I'm sorry."

"About what?" I asked.

"I mixed you and Barry up, sent you to the wrong places. I haven't had that much practice."

"It's okay," I told her. "It worked out. We're both here at the Kendalls' now, and we're none the worse for it."

"Did you—change?" she asked.

"Well, yes."

"Was it bad?"

I thought about it for the first time in hours.

"It was kind of ... disconcerting," I said, "but I don't know that I'd call it *bad*. It was something I had to experience sooner or later, anyway. Besides, Uncle George says he can teach me how to control it. I should probably spend my exchange year here, learning the tricks of the trade."

"Well, I'm glad I didn't get you into a lot of trouble."

I shook my head. "No real trouble. But neither one of us found Dad."

"I know. He's in the darkband," she said. "The guy he had the fight with by the transcomp got away into our band, but Tom managed to shoot him—just a flesh wound, I think—before he transitted out. The darkbander damaged the unit then and—"

"Hold on! Hold on!" I said. "How do you know all this?"

"The cleaning service," she said. "They came by after you left."

"But they'd already been—" I began, and then I saw what she meant.

"The first man had to be the darkband agent," she said, "and it was his blood that you smelled. He must have had confederates in town—someone who's been studying us—to have come up with that story to cover his escape. Very thorough—that story was just in case we saw him leaving."

"What did you do? And how did you know the other ones weren't the fakes?"

"I recognized the people in the second group. I'd looked out the window when I heard their truck pull up. It was the same one they always use. We'd never seen a truck for the first man, and I didn't recognize his name or his voice. I told the second ones the story you'd made up about the remodeling. And I remembered what you'd said about blood. So after they left I turned on the lights and looked around. I found some dried bloodstains on the back steps and a bloody handkerchief in the parking lot."

"Why do you think he came through and attacked Dad?"

"I don't know," she said. "I have no idea exactly what he wanted. But I'll bet it has something to do with the war in the darkband. It could be that now things have gotten more hectic there, the darkbanders are trying to stir up trouble in the other bands, to keep them from helping the partisans as much as they might."

I pushed her out to arms' length and stared at her face. While I had complained to her a lot about not feeling trusted, as she was making her way toward me through the mist, going on about not being in on secrets that everyone else seemed to know, I had not mentioned every little detail—like the partisans. Now it appeared that she was yet another family member who was in on things that I wasn't.

My teeth made a gnashing noise as I brought them together.

"Jim, what's the matter?" she asked.

"Everybody knows stuff I don't!" I said. "Even you! And you're a lot younger! How come Dad told you all this stuff when he didn't tell me?"

"He didn't!" she cried. "I found out for myself! He didn't even know that I knew at first!"

"What do you mean 'at first'?" I asked.

She hesitated, looking frightened. "Later on, I did tell him some things I'd learned," she said. "That's what I meant."

"So what did he do? What did he say?" I asked.

"He told me to keep them to myself."

"That's all?"

"Uh-huh."

"I don't think so," I said. "You've never been a good liar."

"Well, maybe those weren't his exact words," she replied. "But that's what it amounted to."

"Becky," I said. "Tell me *exactly* what he told you."

She pulled away from me.

"Look, I don't want to talk about it," she answered. "I only mentioned the fighting because you told me how you heard about it when you were talking to me back in the fog. Let's drop it now. Okay?"

"Not okay," I replied. "I want to know. It's making me feel like an outcast. Why doesn't he trust me?"

"He *does* trust you," she said.

"Okay, I'll guess what he said. He didn't just say keep your mouth shut. He said, 'Don't tell Jim.' "

She looked away.

"Didn't he?"

"All right. Yes, he did."

"Why? If he trusts me why is he keeping me in the dark about all this stuff?"

"I can't say," she replied.

"Why not?"

"He made me promise I wouldn't."

I sighed. I slapped the side of a tree. A few guesses might have started tying themselves together in my mind about then.

"His present predicament involves all of this stuff, doesn't it?" I asked.

"Yes, it does," she said.

"In that case," I suggested, "all bets are off.

He's in trouble and he needs help. That would cancel any promises that got made back when he couldn't foresee this. I need the information if I'm going to be of any help to him."

She thought about it, her face going through a whole series of contortions before she spoke.

"The reason he wouldn't tell you anything," she finally said, "is because Agatha's still alive."

Agatha. That's my mother's name.

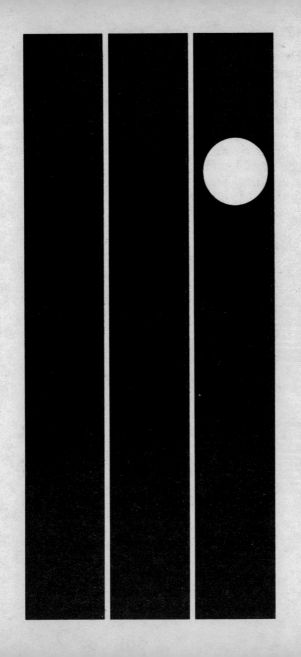

IX

Okay. Back up, Jim. . . . I thought hard and deeply about my mother—a thing I had not permitted myself to do for some time, because we had been very close, and thinking about it made it hurt all over again. She and Uncle George were brother and sister, though there was small resemblance, he being short, sandy-haired, stolid, while she was tall, slim, brunette; also, she was not a shapeshifter, and she lacked George's reticence. She talked more than he did, she touched more, she smiled more. Other relatives used to say that she'd gotten that generation's full share of extroversion and there'd been none left for George and Dalah. But she wasn't empty-headed or frail. She'd taught science and math back home, and she shared her branch of the family's love for the outdoors. Her idea of a vacation involved camping, backpacking, rock climbing, canoeing; she was a very good archer and she was twice Women's Champion in the state pistol competition. I have to admit I was more than a little jealous when she brought Becky home and they grew close in ways I couldn't quite understand.

One day, almost a year ago, she'd gone off on one of those frequent family visits we pay among the bands—the things that really kept us current—and it dragged on for months, much longer than usual. Every time I'd ask about it, Dad would say something like "Things keep coming up. Not to worry." But of course, I did worry, because he seemed more and more troubled himself each time he said it. Then the last time I asked, he looked away and was silent for a while. I was almost about to repeat it when he finally spoke. "There's been an accident. She won't be coming back." Whenever I'd press for details he'd just say "I don't want to talk about it," or "There's nothing more to say," or "Leave it at that." When he didn't want to discuss something he could make Uncle George seem like the soul of loquacity.

So while I'd lacked details, I was given to believe that my mother was dead. Why would anybody create such an impression if it were untrue?

I stared at Becky, my rival, my partner in whatever loss or gain this brought our way, and thoughts and feelings flashed by too fast for me to categorize.

"I don't understand," I said at last. "It's bad enough not to tell me what's going on. But to deliberately mislead me . . . How come you knew and I didn't?"

She started walking toward a fallen tree. I fell into step beside her.

"Tom tried telling me the same story he told you," she said. "But I discovered a bit later that it wasn't true, and I told him so. That's when he told me not to tell you."

"Did he say why?"

"Yes. He felt you would figure the way to go to her to try to help, and that you would jeopardize the mission. He said this was the only way of handling the situation, and if everything worked out well you'd have a pleasant surprise."

"And if it didn't I already believed the worst, huh? She's with the partisans, isn't she?"

"Yes. I don't think Tom liked the idea much more than we do, but I don't think he had any choice. She decided to go over while she was on that last trip."

"Why?"

"A whole group of volunteers was going, from all of the lightbands. Most of them were specialists, possessing skills that would be useful—"

"Weapons," I said.

"Well, yes. That too, I guess. But there was more. That darkband had been the place where she and her sister had done their exchange time. She speaks the language and she likes the place a lot, and her sister had married and stayed there, and—"

"I didn't make the connection," I said. "I knew the business about Dalah, but I didn't realize it was that band. She pointed it out to you, though, huh?"

"As part of something else," she explained, coming up beside the fallen tree and seating herself on it. I only realized at that moment just how tired she looked. I sat down beside her and began breaking off twigs, snapping them into smaller and smaller pieces. "It wasn't just her knowledge of weapons they needed," she went on. "That was really sort of secondary."

"What, then?"

"Well . . . the reason she took me in. We're the same. You understand?"

I thought that I did, but I didn't quite know how to say it. In such cases simple and direct usually seems best, though. "You mean, my mother's a witch?" I asked.

She shrugged.

"She never much liked that word," Becky answered. "It has a special meaning in terms of membership in an early folk religion, and we're not really members. No. We're both sensitive to certain forces, though, which is why she was happy to find me. She wanted someone to pass the traditions along to."

"What should I call you, then?"

"Anything you want, I guess. In some places they use the word 'sorceress'. Tom knows, of course. But we do have a tradition of secrecy, and it's especially important to keep the darkbanders from knowing where we all are. They'd try to get rid of us pretty quick if they found out, the way they did with Granny. They don't like us."

"Why not?"

"Because they don't understand us and because we can hurt them. Almost all of us are on the lightbanders' side."

We sat silent for a time; then she began again. "Recently the partisans liberated several large areas, and the people there joined them. They've got a couple of armies now, and they're moving again. We think a turning point's been reached, that the fate of the band will be decided pretty soon."

"Like I said, I've heard parts of this," I told her, "just today. But I didn't realize things were that close to some sort of resolution. I guess that explains the troops in the front yard. I suppose that even more could be on the way. I'll bet the lightbands are getting ready to send help."

"They are," she said, "with special objectives."

"Soon too, I'd guess."

She nodded.

"Soon," she agreed.

I threw away a final twig.

"How is it that you know so much?" I finally said.

"Agatha tells me these things," she said, "when I talk to her. Some of the other things I can see for myself while they're happening—and sometimes before they happen."

"So you've really been talking to Mom?"

"Uh-huh. There are ways we can sometimes reach each other."

"That business with the candles?"

"Sort of," she replied.

"When was the last time you were in touch with her?"

"During the night. I tried going to her first, but she wouldn't let me come through. She barred the path. Then I decided I'd better come here. But I was so tired I started to lose my way."

"Was she . . . all right?"

"I think so. But they're in some kind of trouble. I can't tell exactly what it is yet, but I'm working on it. There's something they've got to do, but they're blocked."

"Are they in danger?"

"I think so."

"What should we do?"

"I don't know yet. I've got to learn the problem first."

"I think we'd better go tell Uncle George and Aunt Maryl everything you've told me."

"Not yet," she said. "They already know what to do when the time comes, but they can't do anything yet, because they're blocked. . . . Of course!"

She looked up and smiled.

"What?" I asked.

"Blocks! Blocks!" she said. "I think that might be what's the matter. But I've got to look and see."

"You've lost me."

"It's all right," she said. "Listen, Jim. I'm going to need some help."

"What can I do?"

"Go and get me some food. I'm hungry. And bring me an empty bowl, too, a clean one."

"Why don't you just come back to the house and eat?"

"No!" she said. "Then we'd be in trouble. They might be able to stop us, because they know what I am."

"Stop us? From doing what?"

"I'm not sure yet. I'll tell you later. But whatever you do, don't let anyone know I'm here."

I glanced at the cloudy sky beyond the stirring tree limbs.

"Could rain," I said.

"Then I'll get wet," she stated. "You won't tell, will you?"

"Why should I tell anybody anything?" I answered.

Uncle George found me while I was searching the pantry for some food and the bowl. When he asked me what I was doing I answered truthfully, "Just looking for something to eat."

"Well, when you finish I'd like to talk to you in the library," he said.

This was it! I thought. He was finally going to fill me in as to what was going on. At last I was going to pick up those details I hadn't yet guessed or learned.

"Let's go now," I said. "I'll grab something to eat afterwards."

He nodded and turned away. I followed him.

I was wrong. What followed was not at all a briefing on the darkband war or the fate of my parents. Instead, he had decided that it was time for my first full-scale lesson in werewolfery. Not that it wasn't fascinating. In fact, I got very engrossed in his explanation and demonstrations. I learned that a true shapeshifter can do it on purpose and does not need a full moon. I also learned that the wolf form, while easiest, is not exclusive; almost any shifting about is achievable, within the constraints of mass conservation, after a certain amount of practice. It was so interesting that I lost track of the time and did not realize that a couple of hours had passed, until he concluded and remarked, "Maybe you'll want to skip that snack now, since it's so close to dinnertime."

Instant guilt. I thought of poor Becky, half starved in the grove, waiting for her bowl and her scraps.

"Maybe just a small bite," I said, backing toward the door.

He looked at me strangely, then said, "I thought you'd have some other questions for me."

"Would I have gotten answers to them?" I asked.

"Not yet," he said.

I shrugged. "Didn't think so," I told him.

"Wait," he said, as I began moving again. "There's reasons."

I nodded. "I'm sure," I said. "See you later."

He opened his mouth as if to speak again, apparently thought better of it, and nodded. I turned and ran from the room.

I wondered as I fled whether he had actually been considering telling me more than he'd originally intended. Maybe he felt sorry for me. Maybe . . . What difference did it make? I already knew most of the important things, and I had to hurry. When I reached the pantry I quickly found Becky some bread and cheese and a couple of apples. I wrapped them in a napkin, and I picked up a small bowl, also. While I was doing this I heard a series of brief familiar cries from somewhere out back. I hid the food and the bowl inside my shirt and I departed.

When I stepped outside I saw him in a level area beyond the stables. Barry had removed his shirt and boots and socks and was working his way through a *kata,* the punches and kicks punctuated by an occasional *kiai.* I had to admit that it was a rather pretty performance, but my thoughts were almost immediately elsewhere. That is, to tell him or not to tell him about Becky. On the one hand, I didn't know what she was up to or what it might lead to. On the other, he'd been in this from the beginning and had certainly acted as if he'd wanted to help. I just wasn't certain what I'd do if he decided it was his duty to tell the Kendalls that Becky was here and we were up to something.

What decided me? I sometimes wondered later. Was it that I trusted him? Or that I had to go past him to get to Becky, and he'd be curious where I was headed anyway?

X

So I told Barry about Becky as we walked back to the wood, and about the things I had learned.

"I felt sorry for you," he said, "but Tom told me not to talk about it, and he's the boss."

"I understand," I said.

"He thought you'd fiddle with the darkband till you hit the right frequency," he told me, "and go to her—"

"He was probably right," I said.

"—and screw things up royally for them."

"Maybe that, too," I agreed.

"Anyhow, I'm glad you know now."

I nodded. We were nearing the place where I had left Becky and I was suddenly a bit nervous. I could see the fallen tree, but Becky was nowhere in sight. A moment later, however, I realized that what I had thought to be a rock or a stump was actually Becky, seated on the ground, not moving.

"I'm sorry," I called to her. "I couldn't get away and—"

"I figured that," she said, raising her head. "Bring me the food, and don't step on my design. Hi, Barry."

As we drew nearer, I saw that she had surrounded herself with an elaborate tracery of

121

lines scratched into the earth. A damp-looking stick lay near her right hand, and there was a pile of dry ones off to her left. Barry halted and studied the markings suspiciously. I continued on, picking my way carefully amid the lines, avoiding stepping on any of them. She accepted the napkin of food but handed the bowl back to me.

"Go wash it in the stream," she said. "Then fill it about two-thirds of the way with water and bring it back."

There were a few distant grumbles of thunder as I did this, but no rain followed. I came back with the bowl before Becky had finished eating, and I set it down in front of her, careful not to drip on her artwork. As I watched her eat whatever meal that was for her, I'd a funny feeling that I was going to miss my own dinner. I should probably have brought more.

She handed me the napkin and the apple cores when she had finished.

"Do something with these," she said.

"Okay," I agreed. "Then what?"

"Then you wait," she said. "Over there."

She gestured off in Barry's direction.

As I made my way back I tossed the cores into the woods and folded the napkin and put it in my pocket. I hunkered beside Barry and waited.

"What's she doing?" he whispered.

"Looks like she's just staring into the bowl of water," I said.

This went on for a long while, and finally—I'd known it would come sooner or later—I heard a bell, the dinner bell, ringing. Shortly thereafter I heard my name called, then Barry's. The voice was Aunt Maryl's.

Barry swore softly and glanced at me.

"We can't go," I said.

"I know," he replied. "But what if they come looking for us?"

"We'll just have to wait and see."

Several minutes later she called again. Again, we did not stir. But "Come here," Becky said a little later.

We got to our feet and trod gently amid her drawings. She began speaking then, without standing, without looking at us.

"I see what's happened . . ." she said. "It's a deadlock right now . . ."

"What do you mean?" Barry asked, when the next silence began to grow uncomfortable.

"They're pinned down near a key installation— some sort of power station," she answered. "If they can take control of the place it will be a turning point. They'll have the region. But there's a darkband force they can't get past, holding them in their position. Both sides know how important the situation is. Both sides are waiting for reinforcements. Whichever gets them first is going to win."

The bell rang again. Our names were called again. This time there was a note of exasperation in Aunt Maryl's voice.

"Where are the darkbanders' reinforcements?" I asked.

"On the march, and they're bringing artillery."

"Where are ours?"

"Waiting, in various places all over the light-bands," she replied, and I immediately thought of the troops camped in front of the manor. "But they can't get through to help the rebels."

There came another rumble of thunder, and the wind stirred the trees and shrubs.

"Because the darkbanders are jamming the rebels' transcomp," she said, answering my unspoken question. "They've learned the rebels' frequencies, and they've a machine down in their camp that's blocking them."

"So the darkbanders will win as soon as their help arrives," Barry said.

"Unless their transmitter is destroyed," she replied.

"And we can't transmit more people in to do that because the band is blocked," I said. "It's a Catch–Twenty-two."

"I can get us through," she said softly, "the same way I came here."

"I thought Mom had blocked your way to the band," I said.

"No, she just blocked my way to her. She can't keep me out of a whole damn band."

"Say you can get us there," Barry said. "What good can three kids do against an armed camp? I don't see how we could get near the thing."

"It's already night there," she answered. "I can cloak us in the dark, make us almost impossible to detect—for a while, anyway."

The shrubbery rustled again, and this time there was no wind. Neither of them seemed to notice this and I said nothing. Something troubled me about her proposal, too, though it took me several moments to put my finger on what it was.

"Becky," I said finally, "you're not telling us everything."

She looked up for the first time and met my gaze. I saw that her eyes were wet.

"I've told you everything that's important," she answered. "If I take us through and get us into their camp, and we break the transmitter,

then the partisans' transcomp will start working again. They'll have reinforcements, high
tech and low, pouring in. If that happens before the other side gets reinforced they'll break
out and win the battle. Then they'll attack the
station. It shouldn't be a hard thing to capture
with all the extra help. There's other fighting
going on elsewhere, but this battle is crucial. If
they secure this area it might be the end of the
war, except for the cleaning up."

"I understand all of that," I said, "but it
wasn't what I was talking about. Mom and
Dad are with the rebels. . . ."

"Yes. Tom apparently got through right before the jamming began."

"Well, if Mom's a sorceress with more experience than you, how come she didn't make a
few people invisible and go after the transmitter herself?"

"They're jamming her, too," she said.

"How the hell do you jam a sorceress, Becky?"

"You bring in one of your own to attack
her," she replied. "Then she has to defend herself. They fight each other in their own ways
then, and whoever slips up gets fried. They're
too busy to do anything else. So you have a
deadlock there too."

"I thought the darkbanders didn't have any
people like that."

"They don't have too many, but they do have
a few renegades working with them. They
brought one along on this expedition because
they knew this rebel group had one."

"How long can a duel like that go on?" I
asked.

"Till one of them slips up," she said.

"I mean, how long can Mom keep something like that going?"

"I don't know," she said. "I've never done it. It depends on how strong they both are, and maybe how tricky."

"What I'm getting at," I said, "is that you say you can cover us with some spell or other and get us into the darkband camp. But if they've got a sorceress in there, won't she be able to spot us sneaking in?"

"Sorcerer," she corrected. "Theirs is a man. From around here, I think. But I was counting on him being so distracted by his own problems with Agatha that he wouldn't feel us in the neighborhood. If he does try anything he'll have to break his concentration to do it. Then she'll get him—and I could probably protect us in the meantime."

"If you can take us through," Barry asked, "why can't you bring along all those troops in the front yard? If they were to flank the darkband camp or hit it from the rear the partisans would probably move in. We'd catch them between two forces."

"No," she said. "I'm not that strong. It's a question of large masses as opposed to small ones. I can take a few people through, but not a big group."

"One more question occurs to me," I said. "If you can get us into their camp and we break their machine, how do we, uh, get out again?"

She looked away.

"It will be a question of staying safe till the partisans attack," she said. "We either hide or we run for it, whichever seems the best idea."

"I see," I said, realizing that my mouth had become very dry. I had anticipated her answer some time back. Barry simply smiled and nodded. Mr. Cool. His people love that sort of business—coming back with their shields or on them. They even make up songs about it. As for me, it seemed pretty clear that even if we made it in and did the job, we were all going to die afterward. On the other hand, my parents would probably die if we didn't try. I suppose I should have thought nobly and selflessly about how the fate of an entire band might hinge upon our action. But I'm not that noble and selfless. The place was just an abstraction to me. The only ones I really cared about were my folks. I'm not cut out for sainthood and I think most heroics are stupid.

So, "I can't think of any better ideas," I said.

"Then I think we'd better get going," she answered, "before the rain comes and ruins my keys." She surveyed her designs once again.

"I wish there were some way we could leave a message for Aunt Maryl and Uncle George," I said.

"If we succeed they'll know soon enough," Barry said, producing a pocketknife. "Before we go, though, I want to cut a good sapling and trim it. A staff is a great weapon."

Becky glanced at the lowering clouds.

"Okay, but don't waste any time," she said.

He headed back among the trees and I watched him go. I felt a drop of rain on my hand, another on my cheek. Across from me the shrubbery stirred slightly. Maybe just the wind.

"You're a tough kid, Becky," I said, but she did not answer me. Instead, she began laying out the dry sticks on a nearby part of her pattern. Softly, very softly, she seemed to be singing as she did it.

I watched her for a time. The pattern of sticks she was creating seemed to bear some resemblance to the design she had made with the brass rods when she had sent me here. It wasn't identical, but there was some sort of coherence to the form which struck me as similar to that other one. When she was finished she rocked back on her heels and regarded her work, still voicing that nameless, airy tune. After a small while she began producing a soft clicking noise, and at first I wasn't sure how she was doing it.

A little later Barry came up, a staff in his hands, and stood beside me. His face was even more expressionless than usual, and his gaze seemed a hard, flinty thing.

"All right," he said. "I'm ready."

Becky did not reply at once, but her singing grew louder and the clicking began to occur more frequently, interspersed with a kind of rough, grating sound. I saw then that she was holding two small, smooth river pebbles in her left hand, rolling them back and forth against each other, occasionally clicking them together in counterpoint to her song. Then I became aware of something stirring, something blank and . . .

I jerked my head up and to the left. Then I sighed. It was the fog. It had come back to the place it had occupied earlier, between the trees. Tenuous, drifting at first, it seemed to deepen, to grow more dense, to become more still.

It was only then that I realized that a part of Becky's design extended right on back into that area where the fog hung like some ghostly curtain, and that that part of her drawing seemed most like a path or trail. I felt more raindrops then, and a strong wind came up and blew about us, but the whiteness remained. Becky got to her feet and turned away, indicating that we should follow her and that we should pass through the same areas of her design that she did.

So I fell into step behind her, and Barry followed me. The thing wound around itself like a chambered nautilus, going in a counterclockwise direction. I heard the continued grating of the stones she rolled together, along with her singing, which rose and fell within the wind. The rain was coming down more heavily now, and when we made a final turn I saw that we had come onto that long last stretch which led into the fog. From the corner of my eye I thought I saw something move off to my right. But three more steps and it didn't matter. We had entered the fogbank and the sounds of the storm were suddenly muffled and I no longer felt any raindrops. It was similar to my experience of the other night. We had already come too far to be contained within that small wisp of mist, yet it seemed to stretch on and on for a great distance. The ground had a soft turfy feel to it. Becky's voice seemed somehow altered. I could hear no other sounds than the ones she was making, not even my own breathing.

Again it seemed we walked for a long while in a kind of pearly twilight, though I couldn't see for more than a few feet in any direction. I could see Becky ahead of me, and I followed her; I could sense, rather than hear, Barry's presence at my back. Somehow, I found this reassuring. It was far better to have their com-

pany than it had been walking off alone into
the unknown, as I had the other night.

After a time the white walls receded and
finally vanished. We were walking in a wood,
and it was night. Becky kept going and we
kept following until she finally raised her hand
and halted.

"What is it?" I whispered.

"We're here," she said.

XI

We crouched as Becky parted the foliage to give us a view of what lay before us. Directly ahead was a camp. There were tents and scattered lumps that looked like bedrolls, and a few fires and armed guards lurking about. Far behind it, to our left, was what I assumed to be the partisans' objective, though it didn't resemble any sort of power station with which I was familiar. It was a huge installation surrounded by a wire fence; it was filled with tall, fragile-looking towers, which wore halos of blue light. Lower boxlike structures were situated among the towers, and great dark cables coiled and stretched from one to another, seeming to tie the whole thing together. There seemed to be armed human figures patrolling among these forms.

Far off to our right, beyond the encampment we faced, rose a range of hills. Partly shielded campfires glowed here and there along its middle height. Again, I glimpsed some figures, possibly patrolling that area. Those would be the rebels, it seemed, my parents somewhere among them.

Becky made a small noise while Barry and I were studying the scene. I glanced at her and saw that she was staring far off to the left. I followed her gaze, but I could see nothing unusual at first.

Then, as my vision passed back and forth over that area to the rear of the camp, I spotted some small movements and several big outlines, which were being moved jerkily about.

"It must be their reinforcements," I heard Barry whisper. "It looks as if they're setting up artillery pieces back there."

Becky made another small noise.

"We've got to go in soon," she said.

"They may well save their ammo for daylight," Barry remarked, "when they can see better what they're shooting at."

"Even so," Becky answered, "we can't wait till then. My spell works best at night, and the rebels are going to need reinforcements soon. It will take a while to bring them through and to tell them what they have to do."

"Yeah," Barry said. "So what do we do now?"

"I'm going to need about ten minutes of silence," she replied, "to put our protection together. I'll let you know when it's ready, and then we'll go in."

"Do you know which tent their machine's in?" I asked.

"No," she said. "We'll just have to look."

"I'd guess it would be the one on highest ground," Barry observed, "which would be that big one toward the farther side."

"All right, we'll head for it," she said.

Then we backed away from the place where we had been kneeling until we came to a somewhat more open area. Becky seated herself on the ground. She appeared to be thinking. I sat down to her left, Barry to her right, and we waited. Nothing much happened for a long time, but then suddenly I felt it.

It was as if the woods were somehow more alive all about us, as if the trees were shedding something like gossamer onto us. But it was finer than any spiderweb; it was almost like a breeze with something of substance to it. But there were no real breezes blowing.

When Becky stood and said, "Take my hands," and we did, letting her lead us forward among the trees and out of them, it was almost as if we were wearing veils of some material that didn't quite register on the senses. But now I noted that every light source, like the distant campfires, seemed somehow muted, somehow slightly dimmed, yet in the dark spaces in between, everything seemed to be glistening slightly. It was almost like moonlight, though there was no moon risen.

We did not speak as we advanced upon the camp, but my heart was beating heavily and it seemed a real effort to keep my breathing silent and regular. When we neared the perimeter of the place I half expected some sentry to challenge us, but nothing happened. Surely as we passed the first tent someone would step out and . . .

Nothing happened.

We kept going. We halted a couple of times to let people pass, but no one seemed to notice us. I'd no idea Becky could be that competently professional about anything. I resolved then never to tease her again. The cloaking spell was not a hundred percent effective, I'd gathered, and Becky took us far out of our way to avoid large concentrations of reclining troops. We did pass one man who seemed to be staring right at us. But he only shook his head and rubbed his eyes as we passed. Maybe he was a bit more sensitive than the others. We got out of his vicinity quickly, though.

It occurred to me as we passed along that if the tent we had made our goal were indeed the one we sought, our best chance of surviving after we wrecked the transmitter would be to keep going in the direction we were now headed, in that the tent lay near the farther perimeter of the camp. That area off to the place's left flank was open, and if we could cross it fast there were more trees in the distance.

There came an explosion from far off to the left, to the rear of the camp. Shortly, there was another. Even before the second detonation occurred, however, all three of us must have realized what it was, though we said nothing. They were letting loose some artillery rounds, lobbing shells over the camp and against the hillside. We hurried on. We had to find the thing now, and pretty quickly, too.

As we neared the tent it seemed more and more likely that it was the one we sought. There appeared to be some sort of antenna affixed to the top of one of its main poles, and something that appeared to be a small generator stood humming behind the tent. Becky halted us and we studied the place for some time. There came more explosions from far to the left, and this time they continued fairly steadily. The first few must only have been trials, while this sounded like the beginning of a bombardment.

We discovered that it was impossible for us to communicate in whispers, and we didn't want to try shouting and possibly attracting local attention to ourselves, readily visible or not. There was a sentry leaning on a rifle in front of the tent flap in front. Barry nudged us both, pointed to the man, pointed to himself, and pointed to his staff. Becky and I looked at each other, then nodded. I couldn't think of any other way past the man, for if we went around to the side and cut a hole in the tent it would probably draw attention fast. Becky indicated by gesture that we should all advance together or we'd lose the protection of her spell. Barry nodded, and we moved forward again. The artillery barrage was still in progress and I could see clouds of smoke rising at various points along the hillside. How effective this might be in terms of actual damage I could not tell. From the rhythm of the firing and the sources of the flashes I could sometimes spot, it seemed that there were three field pieces in operation.

As we moved quietly but surely toward the tired-looking sentry, I thought ahead to what was going to happen. I did not doubt that Barry could knock him out quickly, relatively mercifully, and with a minimum of damage. He'd been training at that sort of thing all his life. But I was considering the moment when the man fell. We couldn't just leave him lying there as an advertisement that something was wrong. The only practical thing to do would be to drag him inside immediately. And that would commit us to fast action. Whether we were visible or not, it was going to put anybody on the inside on immediate alert when the trooper came crashing in. If it turned out we were in the wrong tent our entire mission would be messed up. And even if it were the right tent, there was no way of telling how many people might be inside.

Becky halted and put her hands on both of us, indicating pretty clearly that we should stop too. She pushed our heads together and moved so that her mouth was but a few inches from our ears. Then she spoke sharply, piercing the banging of the guns with her words:

"I don't like it! There's something very wrong in that tent!"

"What do you mean?" Barry said carefully.

"I don't know," she answered. "I'm sure it's the right place. But it's—like a trap. I've got this bad feeling of danger."

Barry and I looked at each other. We already knew we were in danger, so it wasn't as if this were any special news. Besides—

"What choice do we have?" Barry asked.

She was silent for several moments, then she nodded.

"But it's something special," she added.

"I don't see how we can be more careful than we already are," I said.

She nodded again and we resumed stalking the guard. Now I found myself wishing the artillery would continue just a little longer, to cover the sounds of the disturbance we were about to create.

As we drew near, the guard began shifting about, glancing in all directions. Several times his gaze slid right over us but did not falter. We continued our approach. Suddenly then, Barry moved. His staff cut an arc so quickly I barely saw it, striking the man behind his right ear. Barry was through the tent flap and inside then, almost before the guard began to fall.

I made a quick decision. Barry almost certainly didn't need any help I might give him, and as I'd decided earlier we had to dispose of the evidence. Therefore, I caught the guard under the armpits and dragged him back and through the tent's entrance—my job, as I saw it. Becky snatched up the rifle and followed. From behind me, within, I heard the sounds of a brief scuffle.

As soon as I had the soldier through the entrance, I lowered him, straightened, and turned to survey the interior. To the rear was a table supporting a unit that bore some resemblance to our transcomp back home. From the lights on its face it appeared to be turned on and functioning. Before it, a brown-shirted man—apparently its operator—was slumped unconscious. Toward the center of the area Barry was attacking a second man, who was defending himself with a shovel. They circled and feinted several times, parrying each other's strikes. Suddenly Barry dropped and caught the man behind the knees with a sweeping movement of his staff. As he fell backward, Barry was already striking again, for the stomach, the neck.

"Very impressive," came a voice from the far side of the tent as the man sprawled and lay still, "for one so young."

Becky had just lowered the rifle to the floor and I was about to head for the machine. But we all turned in the direction of that assured, mocking voice. Its owner flowed to his feet from a cross-legged position atop a bedroll. He was barefoot, and he had on black trousers and a matching shirt open wide at the neck. I could see that some sort of medallion hung amid the hairs of his chest. He was not a large man, slim of build, and perhaps only a few inches taller than Barry. His dark hair was long and tied back in a ponytail, revealing a silver earring in his left ear. His eyes were very dark, and when he raised his hands I saw that he wore several rings on each.

Becky stifled a cry as Barry stepped forward, beginning to spin his staff.

"It's him," she said softly, and I realized suddenly that the artillery had let up moments ago.

"Who?" I said.

"The one I saw . . ."

Just then there came a splintering, cracking sound, and the staff fell apart in Barry's hands. The man stepped forward and Barry threw the two pieces he still held at him. The man brushed them aside with two almost casual gestures and continued to advance, and I realized what Becky had meant. This had to be the darkband sorcerer Mom had been fighting, the one Becky had assured me Mom would nail if his attention wavered. Only now his attention was entirely focused upon Barry and he seemed none the worse for it. This could only mean that Mom had lost, that she might well be dead now and that this man had done it. Suddenly, I wanted to attack him myself, but Barry was already there.

Barry spun suddenly into an attack I'd heard him refer to as a turning back kick. But even as he moved, the sorcerer was already stepping to the side, as if he'd read his mind. His hands seemed to move very slowly and to fall very lightly, but when they touched Barry's extended leg I saw him stiffen. Then Barry fell backward to the ground and lay still.

The man smiled and raised his head. He looked at Becky. He looked at me.

". . . And his name is Crow," Becky said. "Smash the machine!"

Her hands were already drifting upwards as she spoke, and the man's gaze snapped back to her.

"What have we here?" he remarked, his own hands doing the same.

"What happened to Agatha?" she asked.

He looked for a moment as if he were considering whether the truth could hurt him in any way, then he said, "I don't know. Our contact was broken when the firing started. Maybe she was hit. I haven't felt her presence since."

I felt a tension beginning to build between them, as if at some level they were wrist wrestling, their arms swaying back and forth. I began to retreat toward the machine. The man she had named Crow glanced at me, as if he wished to do something to halt me. Almost immediately, however, he winced, and I continued on my way, feeling as if I had just avoided something nasty. My movements were slowed, however.

"You're strong, my dear," he said. "Becky, is it? But you're tired, very tired."

"So are you," she said.

"But I'm stronger, and I know more."

He took a step forward. She retreated a pace. I could see that they were both sweating. I looked about for something to strike the machine with. There was the shovel, but it was too near Crow. Then I decided that the simplest thing to do would be to push it off the table. I set my hands on it and shoved. It didn't budge. Heavy.

All right. Becky was retreating again and Crow advancing as I caught hold of the edge of the table and tried lifting it. It moved a little, but not much. Barry moaned and stirred.

I turned my back on the table and caught hold of its edge again. I bent my knees and squatted. Then I began to straighten my legs.

Becky suddenly retreated all the way to the tent wall, covered her face with her hands and sobbed. Crow laughed.

"Not bad," he said, stepping forward. "But not good enough."

My arms felt as if they were being wrenched out of their sockets as the table rose slowly above the ground. I felt the unit begin to slide along its surface. Crow must have caught the movement because he turned away from Becky immediately and faced me. I knew, somehow, at that moment, that he intended to kill me, and I lifted even harder. Barry was beginning to raise himself slowly from the ground, but he was in no shape to be of any help yet.

It was then that the tent flap moved and a great gray wolf entered and sprang. I thrust with my legs and the table rose and went over and the machine crashed to the ground. Crow was driven face forward into the earth, and I heard the snarls, saw the flash of Uncle George's fangs.

XII

I understand we all died that night and were later buried in the area. But I remember getting out through the opening Uncle George slashed in the far side of the tent and running with Barry's arm across my shoulders, half dragging him, Becky stumbling along to my left, as another artillery barrage let loose. I remember our making it to a place among some trees and collapsing there for a time before we were able to continue to a distant point where the hills began. It was almost morning before we'd climbed, turned to our right, and begun making our way in the direction of the partisans' position. Day broke before we reached it, though, and we saw the lines of attackers flow down the hillsides and begin their advance upon the darkband camp. There seemed to be an awful lot of them, and I detected gear from a number of different bands. The artillery ceased a little later, but all of the other sounds of combat now reached us with great clarity, despite the distance. I don't know how long we watched before the camp was secured, but our troops moved on then to attack the power installation, still dark and flickering, like some city of gnomes uncovered in day's light. The installation was surrendered without a struggle, however. Its defenders, who had been watching the battle, must have decided their cause was hopeless. It was only when I realized that the place was captured that I noticed how warm I had grown and looked up to regard the sun's position. It had moved considerably since daybreak. Several hours must have passed while we watched, though it felt as if we had been standing there for a much shorter time.

We continued on toward what had been the rebels' position the night before, avoiding craters and strewn debris more and more frequently as we came nearer. Uncle George had shifted back to his normal human form by then and appropriated some clothing from a wrecked shelter. I think he smelled my parents at about the same time I did. We raced forward and rounded a stand of stone. My father was seated on the ground, a bandage around his head, his back against a boulder; my mother was sleeping wrapped in a blanket nearby.

Becky and I rushed forward, dropping to the ground between them, reaching. . . . Barry followed more slowly, smiling.

Uncle George regarded his sister, then looked at my father.

"Busy night," he said.

Neither Barry nor Becky had any aftereffects from their encounter with Crow; nor did my mother, other than a general fatigue, not all of which could be blamed on the sorcerer's duel. She told me very quietly why she had thought it best to deceive me as she had concerning her absence. I did not agree with her explanation, because I felt I was old enough to have handled the actual situation.

She nodded when I told her that. Uncle George had already explained to her what we had done.

"No more secrets," she said. "Promise."

What could I say? That I was satisfied? It was a lesson in growing up, that's all.

"I'm just happy you're safe," I told her.

Uncle George explained a bit later how he had suspected during our lesson that something was up, and that he'd resolved to investigate when we'd failed to respond to the summons to dinner. He had assumed his stealthier form and watched us. When we'd departed he had followed us through the design and the fog, having pretty much guessed what was going on when he'd seen that Becky was involved.

Dad grew concerned, though, when he'd heard Becky's story in its entirety. I'd thought he'd be upset about the darkbander getting away, but it was the part about Dr. Wade that really seemed to bother him.

"He definitely mentioned the presence of new material in that file?" he asked.

"Yes," I said. "He was very hot on studying it right away."

Dad stared skyward and made the low growling-humming noises he does when he's doing calculations in his head. Then he said to Mom, "It's sometime in the morning back home. Could be he's still there, especially if he stayed up late."

She nodded.

"I understand. I'm up to it," she said.

They both got to their feet.

"Come on. We'd better hurry."

They hunted up the transcomp machine, and Uncle George agreed to act as operator and see if ours was still receiving. After a few signal tests he claimed that it was. Before I transitted out, he squeezed my shoulder.

"I'll be seeing you for some more lessons one of these days," he remarked.

"I'm sure," I said. "Thanks for everything."

He smiled—the first time I'd ever seen him do that.

We needn't have rushed. Dr. Wade was still asleep when we returned home. This gave us time to clean up—I even shaved again—and to begin preparing a heavy breakfast.

Our timing was pretty good. Dr. Wade was up and about before we were finished. I got sent upstairs next door to invite him to join us. He agreed readily. He seemed to be in an awfully good mood.

"This has been an unusually fruitful visit," he said.

"Oh. Great. See you downstairs," I replied.

He was beaming all over the place during breakfast, and, having bought Dad's explanation involving an accident for the neater but still obvious head dressing he wore (or, at least, pretended to), he tried to get Dad into a discussion about the equations he'd turned up, and something he'd just named a "particlemosaic," which he claimed the formulas justified. I couldn't actually tell whether he was talking about some theoretical concept involving energy levels in particle physics, or whether he was saying that it had some immediate application in either weapons systems or pure energy systems. Becky, Barry, and I ate fast and cleared out quickly, leaving him there having coffee with Dad and Mom.

Later, when I wandered—all right, I was curious—near the doorway, I saw that Dr. Wade was leaning back in his chair with his eyes closed while Mom spoke to him softly and steadily. A little later Dad purged all of the new material from the file.

I still remember the man's words as he departed: "I keep feeling I've forgotten something, but I just can't think what it could be."

"Must not have been very important, then," Dad told him.

The darkband invader had, as I had already guessed, been attempting to sabotage our band by introducing a radical and sophisticated physical concept we were not likely to come up with for a long while yet, just at a time perfect to do maximum damage. It was the timing game again. Perhaps nothing bad would have come of it, but we operated our social engineering program by the same rules as the darkbanders— rules of thumb, in a way, derived from experiences in other bands.

Other bands . . . Like the one we died in.

Parallel worlds seem to be created when a certain key turning point in a band's history is reached. There are some theoreticians who say that every decision that is made results in the creation of a parallel world, that every either-or situation goes both ways, with a resultant infinity of universes. They say, though, that the minor variations produce changes too subtle to be detectable with any equipment we have today. Whatever the truth of the matter, there is only a limited number of bands we have detected and that we are able to tune in, and things have worked themselves out in a variety of ways in these different places. The prin-

ciples which determine just what constitutes a
major turning point in a band's history are
profoundly obscure things. We have very little
idea as to how they operate.

But we were there when it happened. It was
the first time in memory when a new band was
activated.

There is now an additional lightband—the
one where the partisans captured the power
installation, won the war, and drove the darkbanders out.

But there is still a third darkband. There,
according to intelligence reports, the rebels'
transcomp was destroyed by artillery fire and
no relief got through to them. My parents died
during that barrage, having been near the machine. Becky, Barry, and I died in the enemy
camp, along with Uncle George. Whether it
was all Crow's doing or whether he'd had help
from the troops could not be discovered. Personally, I think he would've had to have had
help.

It is a very strange feeling to know that
there is a band where I died. But supposing I
hadn't? I'm sure I'd be getting ready to go to
my rescue.

And if I succeeded? It would be an even
stranger feeling, I suppose, meeting me. What
would I say to myself? And which of us would
really own my stereo tapes?

Or Becky? What would we do with another
Becky? Or Barry? Or if we had two Moms and
Dads?

People are not duplicated this way among
the other bands we can tune in. The bands all
parted from wherever they came, a long, long
time ago, and slowly, subtly, they changed as

they went their own ways. Our theoreticians tell us that there would have been full sets of duplicates initially, as happened here, but that gradually, over the centuries, these would have been smoothed away.

But I wonder about all of the people in the new lightband who know that they have twins living in a conquered country. They will be among the first in the new attempts to free the third darkband, I am certain, and there will doubtless be some very interesting impersonations and encounters. One day I hope to go to it as a lightband and to visit my grave, our graves, with flowers.

I could philosophize, I suppose, about some cosmic balancing of good and evil or some such. But there are more lightbands than darkbands, and philosophical concepts—especially ones involving morality—always get too fuzzy for me too soon. Like I said, I want to be a scientist, and I want to work in those areas of discovery where, in the long run, the facts are always stronger than the guesses.

Speaking of long runs . . .

It's a beautiful night out there, and the moon will be rising soon.

I think I'll go and sing to it.

Other Avon Books by
Roger Zelazny

CREATURES OF LIGHT AND DARKNESS
THE DOORS OF HIS FACE, THE LAMPS OF HIS MOUTH
DOORWAYS IN THE SAND
THE LAST DEFENDER OF CAMELOT
LORD OF LIGHT
ROGER ZELAZNY'S VISUAL GUIDE TO CASTLE AMBER
*(An Avon Books Trade Paperback,
co-authored with Neil Randall)*
UNICORN VARIATIONS

The Amber Novels
NINE PRINCES IN AMBER
THE GUNS OF AVALON
SIGN OF THE UNICORN
THE HAND OF OBERON
THE COURTS OF CHAOS
TRUMPS OF DOOM
BLOOD OF AMBER
SIGN OF CHAOS

Other Avon Books in the
Millennium Series

CHESS WITH A DRAGON
by David Gerrold

THE LEGACY OF LEHR
by Katherine Kurtz

ROGER ZELAZNY is best known for his *Amber* series, published by Avon Books. He has won the Nebula Award three times and the Hugo Award four times, most recently in 1986 for his novella *24 Views of Mount Fuji, by Hokusai.* Many of his short stories, such as "A Rose for Ecclesiastes," are already considered SF classics. He earned his letter in collegiate fencing and now lives in the Southwest with his wife and three children.

LEBBEUS WOODS is an internationally acclaimed visionary architect. After working on the design of the noted Ford Foundation building in New York, he established his own firm, where he won a Progressive Architecture citation for applied research in design. A collection of his architectural drawings, *Origins,* was published in 1986. Mr. Woods currently resides in Manhattan with his wife and collaborator, Olive Bridget Brown.